Henry Cuyler Bunner

Jersey Street and Jersey Lane

Urban and Suburban Sketches

Henry Cuyler Bunner

Jersey Street and Jersey Lane
Urban and Suburban Sketches

ISBN/EAN: 9783743441897

Manufactured in Europe, USA, Canada, Australia, Japa

Cover: Foto ©Andreas Hilbeck / pixelio.de

Manufactured and distributed by brebook publishing software (www.brebook.com)

Henry Cuyler Bunner

Jersey Street and Jersey Lane

JERSEY STREET

AND JERSEY LANE

A TANGLED PATH

CONTENTS

LIST OF ILLUSTRATIONS

JERSEY AND MULBERRY

I FOUND this letter and comment in an evening paper, some time ago, and I cut the slip out and kept it for its cruelty:

To the Editor of the Evening ——.

Sir : In yesterday's issue you took occasion to speak of the organ-grinding nuisance, about which I hope you will let me ask you the following questions: Why must decent people all over town suffer these pestilential beggars to go about torturing our senses, and practically blackmailing the listeners into paying them to go away ? Is it not a most ridiculous excuse on the part of the police, when ordered to arrest these vagrants, to tell a citizen that the city license exempts these public nuisances from arrest ? Let me ask, Can the city by any means legalize a common-law misdemeanor ? If not, how can the city authorities grant exemption to these sturdy beggars and vagrants by their paying for a license ? The Penal Code and the Code of Criminal Procedure, it seems, provide for the

punishment of gamblers, dive-keepers, and other dis-
orderly persons, among whom organ-grinders fall, as
being people who beg, and exhibit for money, and
create disorder.   If this is so, why can the police not
be forced to intervene and forbid them their outrageous
behavior ?—for these fellows do not only not know or
care for the observance of the city ordinance, which
certainly is binding on them, but, relying on a fellow-
feeling of vulgarity with the mob, resist all attempts
made to remove them from the exercise of their most
fearful beggary, which is not even tolerated any longer
at Naples.

R.

NEW YORK, *February* 20th.

[Our correspondent's appeal should be addressed to
the Board of Aldermen and the Mayor.   They consented to the licensing of the grinders in the face of a
popular protest.—ED. EVENING ——.]

Now certainly that was not a good letter to
write, and is not a pleasant letter to read; but
the worst of it is, I am afraid that you can
never make the writer of it understand why it
is unfair and unwise and downright cruel.

For I think we can figure out the personality of that writer pretty easily.   She is a nice
old or middle-aged lady, unmarried, of course;

well-to-do, and likely to leave a very comfortable fortune behind her when she leaves all
worldly things; and accustomed to a great
deal of deference from her nephews and nieces.
She is occasionally subject to nervous headaches, and she wrote this letter while she had
one of her headaches. She had been lying
down and trying to get a wink of sleep when
the organ-grinder came under the window. It
was a new organ and very loud, and its organ-
grinder was proud of it and ground it with all
his might, and it was certainly a very annoying
instrument to delicate ears and sensitive nerves.

Now, she might have got rid of the nuisance
at once by a very simple expedient. If she
had sent Abigail, her maid, down to the street,
with a dime, and told her to say: "Sicka lady,
no playa," poor Pedro would have swung his
box of whistles over his shoulder and trudged
contentedly on. But, instead, she sent Abigail down without the dime, and with instruc-
tions to threaten the man with immediate
arrest and imprisonment. And Abigail went
down and scolded the man with the more vigor
that she herself had been scolded all day on

account of the headache. And so Pedro just
grinned at her in his exasperating furrin way,
and played on until he got good and ready to go.
Then he went, and the old lady sat down and
wrote that letter, and gave it to Abigail to post.

Later in the afternoon the old lady drove

out, and the
fresh air did
her a world of
good, and she
stopped at a
toy store and
bought some
trifles for sister
Mary's little
girl, who had
the measles.
Then she came

home, and after dinner she read Mr. Jacob
Riis's book, "How the Other Half Lives;"
and she shuddered at the picture of the Jersey
Street slums on the title page, and shuddered
more as she read of the fourteen people
packed in one room, and of the suffering and
squalor and misery of it all. And then she

made a memorandum to give a larger check to the charitable society next time. Then she went to bed, not forgetting first to read her nightly chapter in the gospel of the carpenter's son of Nazareth. And she had quite forgotten all about the coarse and unchristian words she had written in the letter that was by that time passing through the hands of the weary night-shift of mail-clerks down in the General Post-office. And when she did read it in print, she was so pleased and proud of the fluency of her own diction, and so many of her nephews and nieces said so many admiring things about what she might have done if she had only gone in for literature, that it really never occurred to her at all to think whether she had been any more just and charitable than the poor ignorant man who had annoyed her.

She was especially pleased with the part that had the legal phraseology in it, and with the scornful rebuke of the police for their unwillingness to disobey municipal ordinances. That was founded partly on something that she had heard nephew John say once, and partly on a general idea she has that the present administration has forcibly usurped the city government.

Now, I have no doubt that when that organ-grinder went home at night, he and his large family laid themselves down to rest in a back room of the Jersey Street slum, and if it be so, I may sometimes see him when I look out of a certain window of the great red-brick building where my office is, for it lies on Mulberry Street, between Jersey and Houston. My own personal and private window looks out on Mulberry Street. It is in a little den at the end of a long string of low-partitioned offices stretching along the Mulberry Street side; and we who tenant them have looked out of the windows for so many years that we have got to know, at least by sight, a great many of the dwellers thereabouts. We are almost in the very heart of that " mob " on whose " fellow-feeling of vulgarity " the fellows who grind the organ rely to sustain them in their outrageous behavior. And, do you know, as we look out of those windows, year after year, we find ourselves growing to have a fellow-feeling of vulgarity with that same mob.

The figure and form which we know best are those of old Judge Phœnix—for so the office-jester named him when we first moved in, and we have known him by that name ever since. He is a fat old Irishman, with a clean-shaven face, who stands summer and winter in the side doorway that opens, next to the little grocery opposite, on the alley-way to the rear tenement. Summer and winter he is buttoned to his chin in a faded old black overcoat. Alone he stands for the most part, smoking his black pipe and teetering gently from one foot to the other. But sometimes a woman with a shawl over her head comes out of the alley-way and exchanges a few words with him before she goes to the little grocery to get a loaf of bread, or a half-pint of milk, or to make that favorite purchase of the poor —three potatoes, one turnip, one

carrot, four onions, and the handful of kale
—a " b'ilin'." And there is also another old
man, a small and bent old man, who has some
strange job that occupies odd hours of the
day, who stops on his way to and from work
to talk with the Judge. For hours and hours
they talk together, till one wonders how in the
course of years they have not come to talk
themselves out. What can they have left to
talk about ? If they had been Mezzofanti and
Macaulay, talking in all known languages on
all known topics, they ought certainly to have
exhausted the resources of conversation long
before this time.

Judge Phœnix must be a man of independ-
ent fortune, for he toils not, neither does he
spin, and the lilies of the field could not lead a
more simple vegetable life, nor stay more
contentedly in one place. Perhaps he owns
the rear tenement. I suspect so, for he must
have been at one time in the labor-contract
business. This, of course, is a mere guess,
founded upon the fact that we once found the
Judge away from his post and at work. It
was at the time they were repaving Broadway

with the great pavement. We discovered the
Judge at the corner of Bleecker Street perched
on a pile of dirt, doing duty as sub-section
boss. He was talking to the drivers of the
vehicles that went past him, through the half-
blockaded thoroughfare, and he was addressing
them, after the true professional contractor's
style, by the names of their loads.

" Hi there, sand," he would cry, " git along
lively! Stone, it's you the boss wants on the
other side of the street! Dhry-goods, there's
no place for ye here; take the next turn!"
It was a proud day for the old Judge, and I
have no doubt that he talks it over still with
his little bent old crony, and boasts of vain
deeds that grow in the telling.

Judge Phœnix is not, however, without
mute company. Fair days and foul are all one
to the Judge, but on fair days his companion
is brought out. In front of the grocery is a
box with a sloping top, on which are little
bins for vegetables. In front of this box,
again, on days when it is not raining or snow-
ing, a little girl of five or six comes out of the
grocery and sets a little red chair. Then she

brings out a smaller girl yet, who may be two
or three, a plump and puggy little thing; and

down in the red
chair big sister
plunks little sis-
ter, and there
till next meal-
time little sister
sits and never so
much as offers
to move. She
must have been
trained to this
unchildlike self-
imprisonment, for she is lusty and strong
enough. Big sister works in the shop, and once
in a while she comes out and settles little sister
more comfortably in her red chair; and then
little sister has the sole moment of relief from
a monotonous existence. She hammers on
big sister's face with her fat little hands, and
with such skill and force does she direct the
blows that big sister often has to wipe her
streaming eyes. But big sister always takes it
in good part, and little sister evidently does it,

not from any lack of affection, but in the way
of healthy exercise. Then big sister wipes
little sister's nose and goes back into the shop.
I suppose there is some compact between
them.

Of course there is plenty of child life all up
and down the sidewalk on both sides, although
little sister never joins in it. My side of the
street swarms with Italian children, most of
them from Jersey Street, which is really not a
street, but an alley. Judge Phœnix's side is
peopled with small Germans and Irish. I
have noticed one peculiar thing about these
children : they never change sides. They play
together most amicably in the middle of the
street or in the gutter, but neither ventures
beyond its neutral ground.

Judge Phœnix and little sister are by far
the most interesting figures to be seen from
my windows, but there are many others whom
we know. There is the Italian barber whose
brother dropped dead while shaving a cus-
tomer. You would never imagine, to see the
simple and unaffected way in which he comes
out to take the air once in a while, standing on

the steps of his basement, and twirling his tin-backed comb in idle thought, that he had had such a distinguished death in his family.   But I don't let him shave me.

Then there is Mamie, the pretty girl in the window with the lace-curtains, and there is her epileptic brother.   He is insane, but h a r m l e s s , and amusing, although rather try-ing to the nerves.   He comes out of the house in a hurry, walks quickly up the street for t w e n t y or thirty feet, then turns suddenly, as if he had forgotten something, and hurries back, to reappear two minutes later from the basement door, only to hasten wildly in another direc-tion, turn back again, plunge into the base-ment door, emerge from the upper door, get half way down the block, forget it again, and go back to make a new combination of doors and exits.   Sometimes he is ten or twenty minutes in the house at one time.   Then we suppose he is having a fit.   Now, it seems to me that that modest retirement shows consideration and thoughtfulness on his part.

In the window next to Mamie's is a little, putty-colored face, and a still smaller white face, that just peeps over the sill. One belongs to the mulatto woman's youngster. Her mother goes out scrubbing, and the little girl is alone all day. She is so much alone, that the sage-green old bachelor in the second den from mine could not stand it, last Christmas time, so he sent her a doll on the sly. That's the other face.

Then there is the grocer, who is a groceress, and the groceress's husband. I wish that man to understand, if his eye ever falls upon this page—for wrapping purposes, we will say—that, in the language of Mulberry Street, I am on to him. He has got a job recently, driving a bakery wagon, and he times his route so that he can tie up in front of his wife's grocery every day at twelve o'clock, and he puts in a solid hour of his employer's time helping his wife through the noonday rush. But he need not fear. In the interests of the higher morality I suppose I ought to go and tell his em-

ployer about it.   But I won't.   My morals are
not that high.

Of course we have many across-the-street
friends, but I cannot tell you of them all.   I
will only mention the plump widow who keeps
the lunch-room and bakery on the Houston
Street corner, where the boys go for their
luncheon.   It is through her that many interesting details of personal gossip find their way
into this office.

Jersey Street, or at least the rear of it,
seems to be given up wholly to the Italians.

The most charming tenant
of Jersey S t r e e t is the
lovely Italian girl, who
looks like a Jewess, whose
mission in life seems to be
to hang all day long out
of her window and watch
the doings in the little
stone-flagged courts below
her.   In one of these an
old man sometimes comes out, sits him down
in a shady corner, and plays on the Italian bag-
pipes, which are really more painful than any

hand-organ that ever was made. After a while his wife opens hostilities with him from her window. I suppose she is reproaching him for an idle devotion to art, but I cannot follow the conversation, although it is quite loud enough on both sides. But the handsome Italian girl up at the window follows the changes of the strife with the light of the joy of battle in her beautiful dark eyes, and I can tell from her face exactly which of the old folk is getting the better of it.

But though the life of Jersey and Mulberry Streets may be mildly interesting to outside spectators who happen to have a fellow-feeling of vulgarity with the mob, the mob must find it rather monotonous. Jersey Street is not only a blind alley, but a dead one, so far as outside life is concerned, and Judge Phœnix and little sister see pretty much the same old two-and-sixpence every day. The bustle and clamor of Mulberry Bend are only a few blocks below them, but the Bend is an exclusive slum; and Police Headquarters—the Central Office—is a block above, but the Central Office deals only with the refinements of artistic

2

crime, and is not half so interesting as an ordinary police station. The priests go by from the school below, in their black robes and tall silk hats, always two by two, marching with brisk, business-like tread. An occasional drunken man or woman wavers along, but generally their faces and their conditions are both familiar. Sometimes two men hurry by, pressing side by side. If you have seen that peculiar walk before you know what it means. Two light steel rings link their wrists together. The old man idly watches them until they disappear in the white marble building on the next block. And then, of course, there is always a thin stream of working folk going to and fro upon their business.

In spring and in fall things brighten a little. Those are the seasons of processions and religious festivals. Almost every day then, and sometimes half a dozen times in a day, the Judge and the baby may see some Italian society parading through the street. Fourteen proud sons of Italy, clad in magnificent new uniforms, bearing aloft huge silk banners, strut magnificently in the rear of a German

band of twenty-four pieces, and a drum-corps
of a dozen more. Then, too, come the religious processions, when the little girls are taken
to their first communion. Six sturdy Italians
struggle along under the weight of a mighty
temple or pavilion, all made of colored candles
—not the dainty little pink trifles with rosy
shades of perforated paper, that light our old
lady's dining-table—but the great big candles
of the Romish Church (a church which, you
may remember, is much affected of the mob,
especially in times of suffering, sickness, or
death); mighty candles, six and eight feet tall,
and as thick as your wrist, of red and blue and
green and yellow, arranged in artistic combina-
tions around a statue of the Virgin. From this
splendid structure silken ribbons stream in all
directions, and at the end of each ribbon is a
little girl—generally a pretty little girl—in a
white dress bedecked with green bows. And
each little girl leads by the hand one smaller
than herself, sometimes a toddler so tiny that
you marvel that it can walk at all. Some of
the little ones are bare-headed, but most of
them wear the square head-cloth of the Italian

peasant, such as their mothers and grand-
mothers wore in Italy. At each side of the
girls marches an escort of proud parents, very
much mixed up with the boys of the families,
who generally appear in their usual street
dress, some of them showing through it in

conspicuous places.
And before and be-
hind them are bands
and drum-corps, and
societies with ban-
ners, and it is all a
blare of martial mu-
sic and primary col-
ors the whole length
of the street.

But these are Mul-
berry Street's brief
carnival seasons, and
when their splendor is departed the block re-
lapses into workaday dulness, and the procession that marches and counter-marches before
Judge Phœnix and little sister in any one of
the long hours between eight and twelve and
one and six is something like this:

Up.	Down.
Detective taking prisoner to Central Office.	
	Chinaman.
Messenger boy.	Two house-painters.
Two priests.	Boy with basket.
Jewish sweater, with coats on his shoulder.	Boy with tin beer-pails on a stick.
Carpenter.	
Another Chinaman.	
Drunken woman (a regular).	
Glass-put-in man.	

Up.	Down.
Washerwoman with clothes.	
Poor woman with market-basket.	
	Drunken man.
Undertaker's man carrying trestles.	
Butcher's boy.	
Two priests.	Detective coming back from Central Office alone.

Such is the daily march of the mob in Mulberry Street near the mouth of Jersey's blind alley, and such is its outrageous behavior as observed by a presumably decent person from the windows of the big red-brick building across the way.

Suddenly there is an explosion of sound under the decent person's window, and a hand-organ starts off with a jerk like a freight train on a down grade, that joggles a whole string of crashing notes. Then it gets down to work, and its harsh, high-pitched, metallic drone makes the street ring for a moment. Then it is temporarily drowned by a chorus of shrill, small voices. The person—I am afraid his decency begins to drop off him here—leans on his broad window-sill and looks out. The street is filled with children of every age, size, and nationality; dirty children, clean children, well-dressed children, and children in rags, and for every one of these last two classes put together a dozen children who are neatly and cleanly but humbly clad — the children of the self-respecting poor. I do not know where they have all swarmed from. There were only

three or four in sight just before the organ
came; now there are several dozen in the
crowd, and the crowd is growing. See, the
women are coming out in the rear tenements.
Some male passers-by line up on the edge of
the sidewalk and look on with a superior air.
The Italian barber has come all the way up
his steps, and is sitting on the rail. Judge
Phœnix has teetered forward at least half a
yard, and stands looking at the show over the
heads of a little knot of women hooded with
red plaid shawls. The epileptic boy comes
out on his stoop and stays there at least three
minutes before the area-way swallows him.
Up above there is a head in almost every case-
ment. Mamie is at her window, and the little
mulatto child at hers. There are only two
people who do not stop and look on and
listen. One is a Chinaman, who stalks on
with no expression at all on his blank face;
the other is the boy from the printing-office
with a dozen foaming cans of beer on his long
stick. But he does not leave because he wants
to. He lingers as long as he can, in his passage through the throng, and disappears in the

printing-house doorway with his head screwed half way around on his shoulders. He would linger yet, but the big foreman would call him

"Spitzbube!" and would cuff his ears.

The children are dancing. The organ is playing "On the Blue Alsatian Mountains," and the little heads are bobbing up and down to it in time as true as ever was kept. Watch the little things! They are really waltzing. There is a young one of four years old. See her little worn shoes take the step and keep it! Dodworth or DeGarmo could not have taught her better. I wonder if either of them ever had so young a pupil. And she is dancing with a girl twice her size. Look at that ring of children—all girls—waltzing round hand in hand! How is that for a ladies' chain? Well,

THE CHILDREN ARE DANCING.   THE ORGAN IS PLAYING "ON THE
BLUE ALSATIAN MOUNTAINS"

well, the heart grows young to see them.
And now look over to the grocery. Big sister
has come out and climbed on the vegetable-
stand, and is sitting in the potatoes with little
sister in her lap. Little sister waves her fat,
red arms in the air and shrieks in babyish
delight. The old women with the shawls over
their heads are talking together, crooning over
the spectacle in their Irish way:

" 'Thot's me Mary Ann, I was tellin' ye
about, Mrs. Rafferty, dancin' wid the little
one in the green apron."

" It's a foine sthring o' childher ye have,
Mrs. Finn!" says Mrs. Rafferty, nodding her
head as though it were balanced on wires.
And so the dance goes on.

In the centre of it all stands the organ-
grinder, swarthy and black-haired. He has a
small, clear space so that he can move the one
leg of his organ about, as he turns from side
to side, gazing up at the windows of the brick
building where the great wrought-iron griffins
stare back at him from their lofty perches.
His anxious black eyes rove from window to
window. The poor he has always with him,

but what will the folk who mould public opinion in great griffin-decorated buildings do for him ?

I think we will throw him down a few nickels. Let us tear off a scrap of newspaper. Here is a bit from the society column of the *Evening* ——. That will do excellently well. We will screw the money up in that, and there it goes, *chink !* on the pavement below. There, look at that grin! Wasn't it cheap at the price ?

I wish he might have had a monkey to come up and get the nickels. We shall never see the organ-grinder's monkey in the streets of New York again. I see him, though. He comes out and visits me where I live among the trees, whenever the weather is not too cold to permit him to travel with his master. Sometimes he comes in a bag, on chilly days; and my own babies, who seem to be born with the fellow-feeling of vulgarity with the mob, invite him in and show him how to warm his cold little black hands in front of the kitchen range.

I do not suppose, even if it were possible to

get our good old maiden lady to come down
to Mulberry Street and sit at my window when
the organ-grinder comes along, she could ever
learn to look at the mob with friendly, or at
least kindly, eyes; but I think she would learn
—and she is cordially invited to come—that it
is not a mob that rejoices in "outrageous behavior," as some other mobs that we read of
have rejoiced—notably one that gave a great
deal of trouble to some very "decent people"
in Paris toward the end of the last century.
And I think that she even might be induced to
see that the organ-grinder is following an honest trade, pitiful as it be, and not exercising
a "fearful beggary." He cannot be called a
beggar who gives something that to him, and
to thousands of others, is something valuable,
in return for the money he asks of you. Our
organ-grinder is no more a beggar than is my
good friend Mr. Henry Abbey, the honestest
and best of operatic impresarios. Mr. Abbey
can take the American opera house and hire
Mr. Seidl and Mr. —— to conduct grand opera
for your delight and mine, and when we can
afford it we go and listen to his perfect music,

and, as our poor contributions cannot pay for
it all, the rich of the land meet the deficit.
But this poor, foot-sore child of fortune has
only his heavy box of tunes and a human
being's easement in the public highway. Let
us not shut him out of that poor right because
once in a while he wanders in front of our
doors and offers wares that offend our finer
taste. It is easy enough to get him to betake
himself elsewhere, and, if it costs us a few
cents, let us not ransack our law-books and
our moral philosophies to find out if we cannot
indict him for constructive blackmail, but consider the nickel or the dime a little tribute to
the uncounted weary souls who love his strains
and welcome his coming.

For the editor of the *Evening* —— was
wrong when he said that the Board of Aldermen and the Mayor consented to the licensing
of the organ-grinder " in the face of a popular
protest." There was a protest, but it was not
a popular protest, and it came face to face
with a demand that *was* popular. And the
Mayor and the Board of Aldermen did rightly,
and did as should be done in this American

land of ours, when they granted the demand
of the majority of the people, and refused to
heed the protest of a minority.   For the
people who said YEA on this question were as
scores of thousands or hundreds of thousands
to the thousands of people who said NAY; and
the vexation of the few hangs light in the
balance against even the poor scrap of joy
which was spared to innumerable barren lives.

And so permit me to renew my invitation
to the old lady.

TIEMANN'S TO TUBBY HOOK

TIEMANN'S TO TUBBY HOOK

IF you ever were a decent, healthy boy, or
if you can make believe that you once
were such a boy, you must remember that you
were once in love with a girl a great deal older
than yourself. I am not speaking of the big
school-girl with whom you thought you were
in love, for one little while—just because she
wouldn't look at you, and treated you like a
little boy. *She* had, after all, but a tuppenny
temporary superiority to you; and, after all,
in the bottom of your irritated little soul, you
knew it. You knew that, proud beauty that
she was, she might have to lower her colors to
her little sister before that young minx got
into the first class and—comparatively—long
dresses.

No, I am talking of the girl you loved who

was not only really grown up and too old for
you, but grown up almost into old-maid-
hood, and too old perhaps for anyone. She
was not, of course, quite an old maid, but she
was so nearly an old maid as to be out of all
active competition with her juniors—which

permitted her to
be her natural,
simple self, and
to show you the
real charm of her
w o m a n h o o d.
Neglected by the
men, not yet old

enough to take to coddling young girls after
the manner of motherly old maids, she found
a hearty and genuine pleasure in your boyish
friendship, and you—you adored her. You
saw, of course, as others saw, the faded dulness of her complexion; you saw the wee
crow's-feet that gathered in the corners of her
eyes when she laughed; you saw the faint
touches of white among the crisp little curls
over her temples; you saw that the keenest
wind of Fall brought the red to her cheeks

only in two bright spots, and that no soft
Spring air would ever bring her back the rosy,
pink flush of girlhood: you saw these things
as others saw them—no, indeed, you did not;
you saw them as others could not, and they
only made her the more dear to you. And
you were having one of the best and most
valuable experiences of your boyhood, to
which you may look back now, whatever life
has brought you, with a smile that has in it
nothing of regret, of derision, or of bitterness.

Suppose that this all happened long ago—
that you had left a couple of quarter-posts of
your course of three-score-years-and-ten between that young lover and your present self;
and suppose that the idea came to you to seek
out and revisit this dear faded memory. And
suppose that you were foolish enough to act
upon the idea, and went in search of her and
found her—not the wholesome, autumn-
nipped comrade that you remembered, a
shade or two at most frostily touched by the
winter of old age—but a berouged, beraddled,
bedizened old make-believe, with wrinkles
plastered thick, and skinny shoulders dusted

white with powder—ah me, how you would wish you had not gone!

And just so I wished that I had not gone, when, the other day, I was tempted back to revisit the best beloved of all the homes of my nomadic boyhood.

I remembered four pleasant years of early youth when my lot was cast in a region that was singularly delightful and grateful and lovable, although the finger of death had already touched its prosperity and beauty beyond all requickening.

It was a fair countryside of upland and plateau, lying between a majestic hill-bordered river and an idle, wandering, marshy, salt creek that flowed almost side by side with its nobler companion for several miles before they came together at the base of a steep, rocky height, crowned with thick woods. This whole country was my playground, a strip some four or five miles long, and for the most of the way a mile wide between the two rivers, with the rocky, wooded eminence for its northern boundary.

In the days when the broad road that led

from the great city was a famous highway, it
had run through a country of comfortable
farm-houses and substantial old-fashioned
mansions standing in spacious grounds of
woodland and meadow. These latter occupied the heights along the great river, like a
lofty breastwork of aristocracy, guarding the
humbler tillers of the soil in the more sheltered
plains and hollows behind them. The extreme
north of my playground had been, within my
father's easy remembering, a woodland wild
enough to shelter deer; and even in my boyhood there remained patches of forest where
once in a while the sharp-eyed picked up gun-
flints and brass buttons that had been dropped
among those very trees by the marauding sol-
diery of King George III. of tyrannical memory. There was no deer there when I was a
boy. Deer go naturally with a hardy peasantry,
and not naturally, perhaps, but artificially, with
the rich and great. But deer cannot coexist
with a population composed of what we call
"People of Moderate Means." It is not in
the eternal fitness of things that they should.

For, as I first knew our neighborhood, it

was a suburb as a physical fact only. As a
body politic, we were a part of the great city,
and those twain demons of encroachment,

Taxes and Assessments, had definitively won
in their battle with both the farmers and the
country-house gentry. To the south, the
farms had been wholly routed out of existence.
A few of the old family estates were kept up

after a fashion, but it was only as the officers of a defeated garrison are allowed to take their own time about leaving their quarters. Along the broad highway some of them lingered, keeping up a poor pretence of disregarding new grades and levels, and of not seeing the little shanties that squatted under their very windows, or the more offensive habitations of a more pretentious poverty that began to range themselves here and there in serried blocks.

Poor people of moderate means! Nobody wants you, except the real estate speculator, and he wants you only to empty your light pockets for you, and to leave you to die of cheap plumbing in the poor little sham of a house that he builds to suit your moderate means and his immoderate greed. Nowhere are you welcome, except where contractors are digging new roads and blasting rocks and filling sunken lots with ashes and tin cans. The random goat of poverty browses on the very confines of the scanty, small settlement

of cheap gentility where you and your neighbors—people of moderate means like yourself—huddle together in your endless, unceasing struggle for a home and self-respect. You know that your smug, mean little house, tricked out with machine-made scroll-work, and insufficiently clad in two coats of ready-mixed paint, is an eyesore to the poor old gentleman who has sold you a corner of his father's estate to build it on. But there it is—the whole hard business of life for the poor—for the big poor and the little poor, and the unhappiest of all, the moderately poor. *He* must sell strip after strip of the grounds his father laid out with such loving and far-looking pride. *You* must buy your narrow strip from him, and raise thereon your tawdry little house, calculating the cost of every inch of construction in hungry anxiety of mind. And then you must sit down in your narrow front-room to stare at the squalid shanty of the poor man who has squatted right in your sight, on the land condemned for the new avenue; to wish that the street might be cut through and the unsightly hovel taken

away—and then to groan in spirit as you
think of the assessment you must pay when
the street *is* cut through.

And yet you must live, oh, people of moderate means! You have your loves and your
cares, your tastes and your ambitions, your
hopes and your fears, your griefs and your
joys, just like the people whom you envy and
the people who envy you. As much as any
of them, you have the capacity for pain and
for pleasure, for loving and for being loved,
that gives human beings a right to turn the
leaves of the book of life and spell out its lesson for themselves. I know this; I know it
well; I was beginning to find it out when I
first came to that outpost suburb of New
York, in the trail of your weary army.

But I was a boy then, and no moderateness
of earthly means could rob me of my inheritance in the sky and the woods and the fields,
in the sun and the snow and the rain and the
wind, and in every day's weather, of which
there never was any kind made that has not
some delight in it to a healthful body and
heart. And on this inheritance I drew such

great, big, liberal, whacking drafts that, I declare, to this very day, some odd silver pieces of the resultant spending-money keep turning up, now and then, in forgotten pockets of my mind.

The field of my boyish activity was practically limited by the existing conditions of the city's growth. With each year there was less and less temptation to extend that field southward. The Bloomingdale Road, with its great arching willows, its hospitable old road-houses withdrawn from the street and hidden far down shady lanes that led riverward—the splendid old highway retained something of its charm; but day by day the gridiron system of streets encroached upon it, and day by day the shanties and the cheap villas crowded in along its sides, between the old farmsteads and the country-places. And then it led only to the raw and unfinished Central Park, and to the bare waste and dreary fag-end of a New York that still looked upon Union Square as an uptown quarter. Besides that, the lone scion of respectability who wandered too freely about the region just below Manhattanville, was apt to get his head most beautifully punched at the hands of some predatory gang of embryonic toughs from the shanties on the line of the aqueduct.

That is how our range—mine and the other boys'—was from Tiemann's to Tubby Hook; that is, from where ex-Mayor Tiemann's fine old house, with its long conservatories, sat on the edge of the Manhattanville bluff and looked down into the black mouths of the chimneys of the paint-works that had paid for its building, up to the little inn near the junction of

Spuyten Duyvil Creek and the Hudson River. Occasionally, of course, the delight of the river front tempted us farther down. There was an iron-mill down there (if that is the proper name for a place where they make pig-iron), whose operations were a perpetual joy to boyhood's heart. The benevolent lovers of the picturesque who owned this mill had a most entrancing way of making their castings late in the afternoon, so as to give a boy a chance to coast or skate, an hour after school closed, before it was time to slip down to the grimy building on the river's bank, and peer through the arched doorway into the great, dark, mysterious cavern with its floor of sand marked out in a pattern of trenches that looked as if they had been made by some gigantic double-toothed comb—a sort of right-angled herring-bone pattern. The darkness gathered outside, and deepened still faster within that gloomy, smoke-blackened hollow. The workmen, with long iron rods in their hands, moved about with the cautious, expectant manner of men whose duty brings them in contact with a daily danger. They stepped carefully about, fearful of injuring the regular impressions in the smooth sand, and their looks turned ever with a certain anxiety to the great black furnace at the northern end of the room, where every now and then, at the foreman's order, a fiery eye would open itself for inspection and close

sullenly, making everything seem more dark
than it was before. At last—sometimes it
was long to wait—the eye would open, and
the foreman, looking into it, would nod; and
then a thrill of excitement ran through the
workmen at their stations and the boys in the
big doorway; and suddenly a huge red mouth
opened beneath the eye, and out poured the
mighty flood of molten iron, glowing with a
terrible, wonderful, dazzling color that was
neither white nor red, nor rose nor yellow, but
that seemed to partake of them all, and yet to
be strangely different from any hue that men
can classify or name. Down it flowed upon
the sanded floor, first into the broad trench in
front of the furnace, then down the long dor-
sals of the rectangular herring-bones, spreading out as it went into the depressions to right
and left, until the mighty pattern of fire shone
in its full length and breadth on the flood of
sand; and the workmen, who had been coax-
ing the sluggish, lava-like flood along with
their iron rods, rested from their labors and
wiped their hot brows, while a thin cloud of
steamy vapor floated up to the begrimed

rafters. Standing in the doorway we could watch the familiar pattern—the sow and pigs, it was called—die down to a dull rose red, and then we would hurry away before blackness came upon it and wiped it clean out of memory and imagination.

Below the foundry, too, there was a point of land whereon were certain elevations and depressions of turf-covered earth that were by many, and most certainly by me, supposed to be the ruins of a Revolutionary fort. I have heard long and warm discussions of the nature and history of these mounds and trenches, and I believe the weight of authority was against the theory that they were earthworks thrown up to oppose the passage of a British fleet. But they were good enough earthworks for a boy.

Just above Tiemann's, on the lofty, protrudent corner made by the dropping of the highroad into the curious transverse valley, or swale, which at 125th Street crosses Manhattan Island from east to west, stood, at the top of a steep lawn, a mansion imposing still in spite of age, decay, and sorry days. The

great Ionic columns of the portico, which
stood the whole height and breadth of the
front, were cracked in their length, and rotten
in base and capital. The
white and yellow paint was
faded and blistered. Be-
low the broad flight
of crazy front-steps
the grass grew rank
in the gravel walk,
and died out in brown,
withered patches on
the lawn, where only
plantain a n d sorrel
throve. It was a sad

and shabby old house enough, but even the
patches of newspaper here and there on its
broken window-panes could not take away a
certain simple, old-fashioned dignity from its
weather-beaten face.

Here, the boys used to say, the Crazy
Woman lived; but she was not crazy. I
knew the old lady well, and at one time we
were very good friends. She was the last
daughter of an old, once prosperous family; a

4

woman of bright, even brilliant mind, un-
hinged by misfortune, disappointment, loneli-
ness, and the horrible fascination which an
inherited load of litigation exercised upon her.
The one diversion of her declining years was
to let various parts and portions of her
premises, on any ridiculous terms that might
suggest themselves, to any tenants that might
offer; and then to eject the lessee, either on a
nice point of law or on general principles, pre- ˬ
cisely as she saw fit.   She was almost invariably successful in this curious game, and when
she was not, she promptly made friends with
her victorious tenant, and he usually ended by
liking her very much.

Her family, if I remember rightly, had distinguished itself in public service.   It was one
of those good old American houses where the
men-children are born with politics in their
veins—that is, with an inherited sense of citi-
zenship, and a conscious pride in bearing their
share in the civic burden.   The young man
just out of college, who has got a job at writing editorials on the Purification of Politics, is
very fond of alluding to such men as " indu-

rated professional office-holders." But the
good old gentleman who pays the young ex-
collegian's bills sometimes takes a great deal
of pleasure—in his stupid, old-fashioned way—
in uniting with his fellow-merchants of the
Swamp or Hanover Square, to subscribe to a
testimonial to some one of the best abused of
these "indurated" sinners, in honor of his
distinguished services in lowering some tax-
rate, in suppressing some nuisance, in estab-
lishing some new municipal safeguard to life
or property. This blood in her may, in some
measure, account for the vigor and enthusiasm
with which this old lady expressed her sense
of the loss the community had sustained in the
death of President Lincoln, in April of 1865.

Summoning two or three of us youngsters,
and a dazed Irish maid fresh from Castle Garden and a three weeks' voyage in the steerage
of an ocean steamer, she led us up to the top
of the house, to one of those vast old-time
garrets that might have been—and in country inns occasionally were—turned into ball-
rooms, with the aid of a few lights and sconces.
Here was stored the accumulated garmenture

of the household for generation upon generation; and as far as I could discover, every member of that family had been born into a profound mourning that had continued unto his or her latest day, unmitigated save for white shirts and petticoats. These we bore down by great armfuls to the front portico, and I remember that the operation took nearly an hour. When at length we had covered the shaky warped floor of the long porch with the strange heaps of black and white—linens, cottons, silks, bombazines, alpacas, ginghams, every conceivable fabric, in fashion or out of fashion, that could be bleached white or dyed black—the old lady arranged us in working order, and, acting at once as directress and chief worker, with incredible quickness and dexterity she rent these varied and multiform pieces of raiment into broad strips, which she ingeniously twisted, two or three together, stitching them at the ends to other sets of strips, until she had formed immensely long rolls of black and white. Mounting a tall ladder, with the help of the strongest and oldest of her assistants, she wound the great tall white columns with these strips, fastening them in huge spirals from top to bottom, black and white entwined. Then she hung ample festoons between the pillars, and contrived something painfully ambitious in the way of rosettes for the cornice and frieze.

Then we all went out in the street and gazed at the work of our hands. The rosettes were a failure, and the old lady admitted it. I have forgotten whether she said they looked " mangy," or " measly," or " peaky;" but she conveyed her idea in some such graphic phrase. But I must ask you to believe me

when I tell you that, from the distant street,
that poor, weather-worn old front seemed to
have taken on the very grandeur of mourning,
with its great, clean, strong columns simply
wreathed in black and snowy white, that
sparkled a little here and there in the fitful,
cold, spring sunlight. Of course, when you
drew near to it, it resolved itself into a bewil-
dering and somewhat indecent confusion of
black petticoats, and starched shirts, and
drawers, and skirts, and baby-clothes, and
chemises, and dickies, and neck-cloths, and
handkerchiefs, all twisted up into the most
fantastic trappings of woe that ever decked a
genuine and patriotic grief. But I am glad,
for myself, that I can look at it all now from
even a greater distance than the highway at
the foot of the lawn.

I must admit that, even in my day, the
shops and houses of the Moderate Means
colony had so fringed the broad highway with
their trivial, common-place, weakly pretentious architecture, that very little of the distinctive character of the old road was left.
Certainly, from Tiemann's to the Deaf and

Dumb Asylum—about two miles of straight road—there was little that had any saving grace of honorable age, except here and there where some pioneer shanty had squatted itself long enough ago to have acquired a pleasant look of faded shabbiness. The tavern and the stage-office, it is true, kept enough of their old appearance to make a link between those days and the days when swarms of red-faced drovers, with big woollen comfortables about their big necks, and with fat, greasy, leather wallets stuffed full of bank-notes, gathered noisily there, as it was their wont to gather at all the " Bull's Head Taverns " in and around New York. The omnibuses that crawled out from New York were comparatively modern—that is, a Broadway 'bus rarely got ten or fifteen years beyond the period of positive decrepitude without being shifted to the Washington Heights line. But under the big shed around the corner still stood the great old George-Washington coach—a structure about the size and shape of a small canal-boat, with the most beautiful patriotic pictures all over it, of which I only remember Lord Cornwallis surrendering his sword in the politest and most theatrical manner imaginable, although the poignancy of his feelings had apparently turned his scarlet uniform to a pale orange. This magnificent equipage was a trifle rheumaticky about its underpinning, but, drawn by four, six, or eight horses, it still took the road on holidays; and in winter, when the sleighing was unusually fine, with its wheels transformed into sectional runners like a gigantic bob-sled, it swept majestically out upon the road, where it towered above the flock of flying cutters whose bells set the air a-jingle from Bloomingdale to King's Bridge.

But if the beauty of Broadway as a country high-road had been marred by its adaptation to the exigencies of a suburb of moderate means, we boys felt the deprivation but little. To right and to left, as we wandered northward, five minutes' walk would take us into a country of green lanes and meadows and marshland and woodland; where houses and streets were as yet too few to frighten away that kindly old Dame Nature who was always so glad to see us. If you turned to the right

—to the east, that is—you found the laurel-
bordered fields where we played baseball—I
don't mean that the fields sprouted with
laurels for us boys in those old days of 29 to
34 scores, but that
the *Kalmia lati-*
folia crowned the
gray rocks that
cropped o u t all
around.   Farther
up was the won-
derful and myste-
rious old house of
Madame Jumel—
Aaron Burr's Ma-
dame Jumel—set
a p a r t from a l l
other houses by its
associations with

the fierce, vindictive passions of that strange
old woman, whom, it seems to me, I can still
vaguely remember, seated very stiff and up-
right in her great old family carriage.   At the
foot of the heights, on this side, the Harlem
River flowed between its marshy margins to

join Spuyten Duyvil Creek—the Harlem with
its floats and boats and bridges and ramshackle
docks, and all the countless delights of a boat-
ing river. Here also was a certain dell, half-
way up the heights overlooking McComb's
Dam Bridge, where countless violets grew
around a little spring, and where there was a
real cave, in which, if real pirates had not left
their treasure, at least real tramps had slept
and left a real smell. And on top of the cave
there was a stone which was supposed to
retain the footprint of a pre-historic Indian.
From what I remember of that footprint I am
inclined to think that it must have been made
by the foot of a derrick, and not by that of an
Indian.

But it was on the other side of the Island,
between the Deaf and Dumb Asylum and
Tubby Hook, and between the Ridge and the
River, that I most loved to ramble. Here
was the slope of a woodland height running
down to a broad low strip, whose westernmost
boundary was the railroad embankment, beyond which lay the broad blue Hudson, with
Fort Lee and the first up-springing of the

Palisades, to be seen by glimpses through the tree-trunks. This was, I think, the prettiest piece of flower-spangled wildwood that I have ever seen. For centuries it had drained the richness of that long and lofty ridge. The life of lawns and gardens had gone into it; the

dark wood-soil had been washed from out the rocks on the brow of the hill; and down below there, where a vagrom brooklet chirped its way between green stones, the wholesome soil bloomed forth in grateful luxuriance. From the first coming of the anemone and the hepatica, to the time of the asters, there was always something growing there to delight the scent or the sight; and most of all do I remember the huge clumps of Dutchman's-breeches—the purple and the waxy white as well as the honey-tipped scarlet.

There were little sunlit clearings here, and I well recall the day when, looking across one of these, I saw something that stood awkwardly and conspicuously out of the young wood-grass—a raw stake of pine wood, and beyond that, another stake, and another; and parallel with these another row, marking out two straight lines, until the bushes hid them. The surveyors had begun to lay out the line of the

new Boulevard, on which you may now roll in your carriage to Inwood, through the wreck of the woods where I used to scramble over rock and tree-trunk, going toward Tubby Hook.

It was on the grayest of gray November days last year that I had the unhappy thought of revisiting this love of my youth. I fol-

lowed familiar trails, guided by landmarks I
could not forget—although they had somehow
grown incredibly poor and mean and shabby,
and had entirely lost a certain dignity that
they had until then kept quite clearly in my
remembrance. And behold, they were no
longer landmarks except to me. A change
had come over the face of this old playground
of mine. It had forgotten the withered,
modest grace of the time when it was middle-
aged, and when I was a boy. It was check-
ered and gridironed with pavements and electric lights. The Elevated Railroad roared at
its doors behind clouds of smoke and steam.
Great, cheerless, hideously ornate flat buildings
reared their zinc-tipped fronts toward the gray
heaven, to show the highest aspirations of
that demoralized suburb in the way of domestic architecture. To right, to left, every way
I turned, I saw a cheap, tawdry, slipshod imi-
tation of the real city—or perhaps I should
say, of all that is ugliest and vulgarest, least
desirable, and least calculated to endure, in
the troubled face of city life. I was glad to
get away; glad that the gray mist that rolled

up from the Hudson River hid from my sight
within its fleecy bosom some details of that
vulgar and pitiful degradation.   One place
alone I found as I had hoped to find it.   Ex-
Mayor Tiemann's house was gone, his conser-
vatory was a crumbling ruin; the house we
decked for Lincoln's death was a filthy tenement with a tumble-down gallery where the
old portico had stood, and I found very little
on my upward pilgrimage that had not experienced some change—for the worse, as it
seemed to me.   The very cemetery that
belongs to old Trinity had dandified itself with
a wonderful wall and a still more wonderful
bridge to its annex—or appendix, or exten-
sion, or whatever you call it.   But just above
it is a little enclosure that is called a park—a
place where a few people of modest, old-fashioned, domestic tastes had built their houses
together to join in a common resistance against
the encroachments of the speculator and the
nomad house-hunter.   I found this little settlement undisturbed, uninvaded, save by a sort
of gentle decay that did it no ill-service, in my
eyes.   The pale dust was a little deeper in the

roadways that had once been paved with lime-
stone, a few more brown autumn leaves had
fallen in the corners of the fences, the clustered wooden houses all looked a little more

rustily respectable in their reserved and sleepy
silence—a little bit more, I thought, as if they
sheltered a colony of old maids. Otherwise it
looked pretty much as it did when I first saw
it, well nigh thirty years ago.

To see if there were anything alive in that
misty, dusty, faded little abode of respectabil-

ity, I rang at the door of one house, and found some inquiries to make concerning another one that seemed to be untenanted.

It was a very pretty young lady who opened the door for me, with such shining dark eyes and with so bright a red in her cheeks, that you felt that she could not have been long in that dull, old-time spot, where life seemed to be all one neutral color. She answered my questions kindly, and then, with something in her manner which told me that strangers did not often wander in there, she said that it was a very nice place to live in. I told her that I knew it *had* been a very nice place to live in.

5

THE BOWERY AND BOHEMIA

THE BOWERY AND BOHEMIA

ONE day a good many years ago an old
gentleman from Rondout-on-the-Hud-
son—then plain Rondout—was walking up
Broadway seeing the sights.   He had not
been in New York in ten or twelve years, and
although he was an old gentleman who always
had a cask of good ale in his cellar in the winter-time, yet he had never tasted the strange
German beverage called lager-beer, which he
had heard and read about.   So when he saw
its name on a sign he went in and drank a
mug, sipping it slowly and thoughtfully, as he
would have sipped his old ale.   He found it
refreshing—peculiar—and, well, on the whole,
very refreshing indeed, as he considerately
told the proprietor.

But what interested him more than the beer

was the sight of a group of young men seated
around a table drinking beer, reading—and—
yes, actually writing verses, and bandying very
lively jests among themselves.   The old gen-

tleman could not help hearing their conversation, and when he went out into the street he
shook his head thoughtfully.

"I wonder what my father would have said

to that ?" he reflected. "Young gentlemen sitting in a pot-house at high noon and turning verses like so many ballad-mongers! Well, well, well, if those are the ways of lager-beer drinkers, I'll stick to my good old ale!"

And greatly surprised would that honest old gentleman have been to know that the presence of that little group of poets and humorists attracted as much custom to good Mr. Pfaff's beer-saloon as did his fresh, cool lager; and that young men, and, for the matter of that, men not so young, stole in there to listen to their contests of wit, and to wish and yearn and aspire to be of their goodly company. For the old gentleman little dreamed, as he went on his course up Broadway, that he had seen the first Bohemians of New York, and that these young men would be written about and talked about and versified about for generations to come. Unconscious of this honor he went on to Fourteenth Street to see the new square they were laying out there.

Perhaps nothing better marks the place where the city of New York got clean and clear out of provincial pettiness into metro-

politan tolerance than the advent of the Bohemians. Twenty-five years earlier they would
have been a scandal and a reproach to the

town. Not for their literature, or for their
wit, or for their hard drinking, or even for
their poverty; but for their brotherhood, and
for their calm indifference to all the rest of the
world whom they did not care to receive into
their kingdom of Bohemia. There is human
nature in this; more human nature than there
is in most provincialism. Take a community
of one hundred people and let any ten of its
members join themselves together and dictate
the terms on which an eleventh may be ad-

mitted to their band. The whole remaining
eighty-nine will quarrel for the twelfth place.
But take a community of a thousand, and let
ten such internal groups be formed, and every
group will have to canvass more or less hard to
increase its number. For the other nine hundred people, being able to pick and choose,
are likely to feel a deep indifference to the
question of joining any segregation at all. If
group No. 2 says, " Come into my crowd, I
understand they don't want you in No. 1,"
the individual replies: " What the deuce do I
care about No. 1 or you either ? Here are
Nos. 4, 5, 6, and 7 all begging for me. If you
and No. 1 keep on in your conceit you'll find
yourselves left out in the cold."

And as it frequently happens to turn out
that way, the dweller in a great city soon
learns, in the first place, that he is less important than he thought he was; in the second
place, that he is less unimportant than some
people would like to have him think himself.
All of which goes to show that when New
Yorkers looked with easy tolerance, and some
of them with open admiration, upon the Bohe-

mians at Pfaff's saloon, they had come to be citizens of no mean city, and were making metropolitan growth.

A Bohemian may be defined as the only

kind of gentleman permanently in temporary difficulties who is neither a sponge nor a cheat. He is a type that has existed in all ages and always will exist. He is a man who lacks certain elements necessary to success in this

world, and who manages to keep fairly even
with the world, by dint of ingenious shift
and expedient; never fully succeeding, never
wholly failing. He is a man, in fact, who
can't swim, but can tread water. But he
never, never, never calls himself a Bohemian
—at least, in a somewhat wide experience, I
have known only two that ever did, and one of
these was a baronet. As a rule, if you over-
hear a man approach his acquaintance with the
formula, " As one Bohemian to another," you
may make up your mind that that man means
an assault upon the other man's pocket-book,
and that if the assault is successful the dam-
ages will never be repaired. That man is not
a Bohemian; he is a beat. Your true Bohemian always calls himself by some euphemistic
name. He is always a gentleman at odds with
fortune, who rolled in wealth yesterday and
will to-morrow, but who at present is willing
to do any work that he is sure will make him
immortal, and that he thinks may get him the
price of a supper. And very often he lends
more largely than he borrows.

Now the crowd which the old gentleman

saw in the saloon—and he saw George Arnold,
Fitz-James O'Brien, and perhaps N. P. Shep-
ard—was a crowd of Bohemians rather by its
own christening than by any ordinary applica-
tion of the word. They were all young men
of ability, recognized in their profession. Of
those who have died, two at least have honor
and literary consideration to-day; of those
who lived, some have obtained celebrity, and
all a reasonable measure of success. Mürger's
Bohemians would have called them Philistines.
But they have started a tradition that will
survive from generation unto generation; a
tradition of delusion so long as the glamour of
poetry, romance, and adventure hang around
the mysteriously attractive personality of a
Bohemian. Ever since then New York has
had, and always will have, the posing Bohemian and his worshippers.

Ten or fifteen years ago the " French Quarter" got its literary introduction to New York,
and the fact was revealed that it was the resort
of real Bohemians—young men who actually
lived by their wit and their wits, and who
talked brilliantly over fifty-cent table-d'hôte

dinners. This was the signal for the would-be
Bohemian to emerge from his dainty flat or
his oak-panelled studio in Washington Square,
hasten down to Bleecker or Houston Street,
there to eat chicken badly *braisé*, fried chuck-
steak, and soggy spaghetti, and to drink thin
blue wine and chicory-coffee that he might
listen to the feast of witticism and flow of soul
that he expected to find at the next table. If
he found it at all, he lost it at once. If he
made the acquaintance of the young men at
the next table, he found them to be young
men of his own sort—agreeable young boys
just from Columbia and Harvard, who were
painting impressionless pictures for the love of
Art for Art's sake, and living very comfortably on their paternal allowances. Any one of
the crowd would think the world was coming
to pieces if he woke up in the morning to wonder where he could get his breakfast on credit,
and wonder where he could earn enough money
to buy his dinner. Yet these innocent youngsters continue to pervade "The Quarter," as
they call it; and as time goes on, by much
drinking of ponies of brandy and smoking of

cigarettes, they get to fancy that they themselves are Bohemians. And when they get
tired of it all and want something good to eat,
they go up to Delmonico's and get it.

And their Bohemian predecessors, who
sought the French fifty-cent restaurants as
their highest attainable luxury—what has become of them ? They have fled before that
incursion as a flock of birds before a whirlwind.
They leave behind them, perhaps, a few of
the more mean-spirited among them, who are
willing to degenerate into fawners on the rich,
and habitual borrowers of trifling sums. But
the true Bohemians, the men who have the
real blood in their veins, they must seek some
other meeting-place where they can pitch their
never-abiding tents, and sit at their humble
feasts to recount to each other, amid apprecia-
tive laughter, the tricks and devices and pitiful
petty schemes for the gaining of daily bread
that make up for them the game and comedy
of life. Tell me not that Ishmael does not
enjoy the wilderness. The Lord made him for
it, and he would not be happy anywhere else.

There was one such child of fortune once,

who brought his blue eyes over from Ireland.
His harmless and gentle life closed after too
many years in direst misfortune. But as long
as he wandered in the depths of poverty there
was one strange and mysterious thing about
him. His clothes, always well brushed and
well carried on a gallant form, often showed
cruel signs of wear, especially when he went
for a winter without an overcoat. But shabby
as his garments might grow, empty as his
pockets might be, his linen was always spot-
less, stiff, and fresh. Now everybody who has
ever had occasion to consider the matter knows
that by the aid of a pair of scissors the life of
a collar or of a pair of cuffs can be prolonged
almost indefinitely—apparent miracles had
been performed in this way. But no pair of
scissors will pay a laundry bill; and finally a
committee of the curious waited upon this
student of economics and asked him to say
how he did it. He was proud and delighted
to tell them.

"I-I-I'll tell ye, boys," he said, in his pleasant Dublin brogue, "but 'twas I that thought
it out. I wash them, of course, in the basin—

that's easy enough; but you'd think I'd be put to it to iron them, wouldn't ye, now? Well, I've invinted a substischoot for ironing —it's me big books. Through all me vicissichoods, boys, I kept me Bible and me dictionary, and I lay the collars and cuffs in the undher one and get the leg of the bureau on top of them both—and you'd be surprised at the artistic effect.''

There is no class in society where the sponge, the toady, the man who is willing to receive socially without giving in return, is more quickly found out or more heartily disowned than among the genuine Bohemians. He is to them a traitor, he is one who plays the game unfairly, one who is willing to fill his belly by means to which they will not resort, lax and fantastic as is their social code. Do you know, for instance, what '' Jackaling '' is in New York? A Jackal is a man generally of good address, and capable of a display of good fellowship combined with much knowledge of literature and art, and a vast and intimate acquaintance with writers, musicians, and managers. He makes it his business to haunt

hotels, theatrical agencies, and managers'
offices, and to know whenever, in his language,
" a new jay comes to town." The jay he is

after is some man generally from the smaller
provincial cities, who has artistic or theatrical
aspirations and a pocketful of money. It is
the Jackal's mission to turn this jay into an
" angel." Has the gentleman from Lockport
come with the score of a comic opera under
his arm, and two thousand dollars in his
pocket ? Two thousand dollars will not go

far toward the production of a comic opera in
these days, and the jay finds that out later;
but not until after the Jackal has made him
intimately acquainted with a very gentlemanly
and experienced manager who thinks that it
can be done for that price with strict econ-
omy.   Has the young man of pronounced
theatrical talent arrived from Keokuk with
gold and a thirst for fame? The Jackal knows
just the dramatist who will write him the play
that he ought to star in.   Does the wealthy
and important person from Podunk desire to
back something absolutely safe and sure in the
line of theatrical speculation?· The Jackal has
the very thing for which he is looking.   And
in all these, and in all similar contingencies,
it is a poor Jackal who does not get his com-
mission at both ends.

The Jackal may do all these things, but he
may not, if he is treated, fail to treat in return.
I do not mean to say at all that Jackaling is
a business highly esteemed, even in darkest
Bohemia, but it is considered legitimate, and I
hope that no gentleman doing business in Wall
Street, or on the Consolidated Exchange, will

feel too deeply grieved when he learns the fact.

But where have the real Bohemians fled to from the presence of the too-well-disposed and too-wealthy children of the Benedick and the Holbein ? Not where they are likely to find him, you may be sure. The true Bohemian does not carry his true address on his card. In fact, he is delicate to the point of sensitiveness about allowing any publicity to attach to his address. He communicates it confidentially to those with whom he has business dealings, but he carefully conceals it from the prying world. As soon as the world knows it he moves. I once asked a chief of the Bohemian tribe whose residence was the world, but whose temporary address was sometimes Paris, why he had moved from the Quartier Latin to a place in Montmartre.

" Had to, my dear fellow," he answered, with dignity; " why if you live over on that side of the river they'll call you a *Bohemian !* "

In Paris the home of wit in poverty has been moved across the Seine to the south side of the hill up which people climb to make pil-

grimages to the Moulin Rouge and the church
of St. Pierre de Montmartre. In New York it
has been moved not only across that river of
human intercourse that we call Broadway—a
river with a tidal ebb and flow of travel and
traffic—but across a wilder, stranger, and more
turbulent flood called the Bowery, to a region
of which the well-fed and prosperous New
Yorker knows very, very little.

As more foreigners walk on the Bowery than
walk on any other street in New York; and as
more different nationalities are represented
there than are represented in any other street
in New York; and as the foreigners all say that
the Bowery is the most marvellous thoroughfare in the world, I think we are justified in
assuming that there is little reason to doubt
that the foreigners are entirely right in the
matter, especially as their opinion coincides
with that of every American who has ever
made even a casual attempt to size up the
Bowery.

No one man can thoroughly know a great
city. People say that Dickens knew London,
but I am sure that Dickens would never have

said it. He knew enough of London to know
that no one human mind, no one mortal life
can take in the complex intensity of a metrop-

olis. Try to count a million, and then try to
form a conception of the impossibility of learning all the ins and outs of the domicile of a

million men, women, and children. I have met men who thought they knew New York, but I have never met a man—except a man from a remote rural district—who thought he knew the Bowery. There are agriculturists, however, all over this broad land who have entertained that supposition and acted on it —but never twice. The sense of humor is the saving grace of the American people.

I first made acquaintance with the Bowery as a boy through some lithographic prints. I was interested in them, for I was looking forward to learning to shoot, and my father had told me that there used to be pretty good shooting at the upper end of the Bowery, though, of course, not so good as there was farther up near the Block House, or in the wood beyond. Besides, the pictures showed a very pretty country road with big trees on both sides of it, and comfortable farmhouses, and, I suppose, an inn with a swinging sign. I was disappointed at first, when I heard it had been all built up, but I was consoled when the glories of the real Bowery were unfolded to my youthful mind, and I heard of the butcher-boy

and his red sleigh; of the Bowery Theatre and
peanut gallery, and the gods, and Mr. Eddy,
and the war-cry they made of his name—and
a glorious old war-cry it is, better than any
college cries ever invented: " *Hi*, Eddy-eddy-
eddy - eddy - eddy - eddy-eddy-eddy-eddy!'" of
Mose and his silk locks; of the fire-engine
fights, and Big Six, and " Wash-her-down!"
of the pump at Houston Street; of what happened to Mr. Thackeray when he talked to the
tough; of many other delightful things that
made the Bowery, to my young imagination,
one long avenue of romance, mystery, and
thrilling adventure. And the first time I went
in the flesh to the Bowery was to go with an
elderly lady to an optician's shop.

> " And is this—Yarrow ?—*This* the stream
> Of which my fancy cherished,
> So faithfully, a waking dream ?
> An image that hath perished !
> O that some minstrel's harp were near,
> To utter notes of gladness,
> And chase this silence from the air,
> That fills my heart with sadness ! "

But the study of the Bowery that I began

that day has gone on with interruption for a good many years, and I think now that I am arriving at the point where I have some faint glimmerings of the littleness of my knowledge of it as compared with what there is to be known. I do not mean to say that I can begin to size the disproportion up with any accuracy, but I think I have accomplished a good deal in getting as far as I have.

The Bowery is not a large place, for I think that, properly speaking, it is a place rather than a street or avenue. It is an irregularly shaped ellipse, of notable width in its widest part. It begins at Chatham Square, which lies on the parallel of the sixth Broadway block above City Hall, and loses its identity at the Cooper Union where Third and Fourth Avenues begin, so that it is a scant mile in all. But it is the alivest mile on the face of the earth. And it either bounds or bisects that square mile that the statisticians say is the most densely populated square mile on the face of the globe. This is the heart of the New York tenement district. As the Bowery is the Broadway of the East Side, the street of its

pleasures, it would be interesting enough if it
opened up only this one densely populated
district. But there is much more to contribute
to its infinite variety. It serves the same pur-

pose for the Chinese colony in Mott, Pell, and
Doyers Streets, and for the Italian swarms in
Mulberry Bend, the most picturesque and
interesting slum I have ever seen, and I am an
ardent collector of slums. I have missed art
galleries and palaces and theatres and cathedrals (cathedrals particularly) in various and
sundry cities, but I don't think I ever missed
a slum. Mulberry Bend is a narrow bend in
Mulberry Street, a tortuous ravine of tall tenement houses, and it is so full of people that
the throngs going and coming spread off the
sidewalk nearly to the middle of the street.
There they leave a little lane for the babies to
play in. No, they never get run over. There
is a perfect understanding between the babies
and the peddlers who drive their wagons in
Mulberry Bend. The crowds are in the street
partly because much of the sidewalk and all of
the gutter is taken up with venders' stands,
which give its characteristic feature to Mulberry Bend. There are displayed more and
stranger wares than uptown people ever heard
of. Probably the edibles are in the majority,
certainly they are the queerest part of the

show. There are trays and bins there in the
Bend, containing dozens and dozens of things
that you would never guess
were meant to eat if you
didn't happen to
see a ham or a
string of sausages
or some other
familiar object
among them. But the color
of the Bend—and its color is
its strong point—comes from
its display of wearing apparel and candy. A
lady can go out in Mulberry Bend and purchase
every article of apparel, external or private and
personal, that she ever heard of, and some that
she never heard of, and she can get them of
any shade or hue. If she likes what they call
"Liberty" colors—soft, neutral tones—she
can get them from the second-hand dealers
whose goods have all the softest of shades that
age and exposure can give them. But if she
likes, as I do, bright, cheerful colors, she can
get tints in Mulberry Bend that you could
warm your hands on. Reds, greens, and yel-

lows preponderate, and Nature herself would own that the Italians could give her points on inventing green and not exert themselves to do it. The pure arsenical tones are preferred in the Bend, and, by the bye, anybody who remembers the days when ladies wore magenta and solferino, and wants to have those dear old colors set his teeth on edge again, can go to the Bend and find them there. The same dye-stuffs that are popular in the dress-goods are equally popular in the candy, and candy is a chief product of Mulberry Bend. It is piled up in reckless profusion on scores of stands, here, there, and everywhere, and to call the general effect festal, would be to speak slightingly of it. The stranger who enters Mulberry Bend and sees the dress-goods and the candies is sure to think that the place has been decorated to receive him. No, nobody will hurt you if you go down there and are polite, and mind your own business, and do not step on the babies. But if you stare about and make comments, I think those people will be justified in suspecting that the people uptown don't always know how to behave themselves like

ladies and gentlemen, so do not bring disgrace
on your neighborhood, and do not go in a
cab. You will not bother the babies, but you
will find it trying to your own nerves.

There is a good deal of money in Mulberry
Street, and some of it overflows into the
Bowery. From this street also the Baxter

Street variety of Jews find their way into the
Bowery. These are the Jew toughs, and there
is no other type of Jew at all like them in all
New York's assortment of Hebrew types,
which cannot be called meagre. Of the Jewish
types New York has, as the printers say, "a
full case."

But it is on the other side of the Bowery that there lies a world to which the world north of Fourteenth Street is a select family party. I could not give even a partial list of its elements. Here dwell the Polish Jews with their back-yards full of chickens. The police raid those back-yards with ready assiduity, but the yards are always promptly replenished. It is the p o l i c e against a religion, and the odds are against the police. The Jew will die for it, if needs b e , but h i s chickens must be killed *ko- sher* way and not Christian way, but that is only the way of the Jews: the Hungarians, t h e Bohemians, the Anarchist Russians, the Scandinavians of all sorts who come up from the wharfs, the Irish, who are there, as every-

where, the Portuguese Jews, and all the rest
of them who help to form that city within a
city—have they not, all of them, ways of their
own ? I speak of this Babylon only to say
that here and there on its borders, and, once
in a way, in its very heart, are rows or blocks
of plain brick houses, homely, decent, respectable relics of the days when the sturdy, steady
tradesfolk of New York built here the homes
that they hoped to leave to their children.
They are boarding- and lodging-houses now,
poor enough, but proud in their respectability
of the past, although the tide of ignorance,
poverty, vice, filth, and misery is surging to
their doors and their back-yard fences. And
here, in hall bedrooms, in third-story backs
and fronts, and in half-story attics, live the
Bohemians of to-day, and with them those
other strugglers of poverty who are destined
to become "successful men" in various
branches of art, literature, science, trade, or
finance. Of these latter our children will
speak with hushed respect, as men who rose
from small beginnings; and they will go into
the school-readers of our grandchildren along

with Benjamin Franklin and that contemptible
wretch who got to be a great banker because
he picked up a pin, as examples of what per-
severance and industry can accomplish.   From

what I remember I foresee that those children
will hate them.

I am not going to give you the addresses of
the cheap restaurants where these poor, cheerful children of adversity are now eating *goulasch* and *Kartoffelsalad* instead of the spaghetti and tripe *à la mode de Caen* of their old
haunts.   I do not know them, and if I did, I
should not hand them over to the mercies of
the intrusive young men from the studios and
the bachelors' chambers.   I wish them good

digestion of their goulasch: for those that are
to climb, I wish that they may keep the gen-
erous and faithful spirit of friendly poverty;
for those that are to go on to the end in fruit-
less struggle and in futile hope, I wish for
them that that end may come in some gentle
and happier region lying to the westward of
that black tide that ebbs and flows by night
and day along the Bowery Way.

7

THE STORY OF A PATH

THE STORY OF A PATH

IN one of his engaging essays Mr. John Burroughs tells of meeting an English lady in Holyoke, Mass., who complained to him that there were no foot-paths for her to walk on, whereupon the poet-naturalist was moved to an eloquent expression of his grief over America's inferiority in the foot-path line to the "mellow England" which in one brief month had won him for her own. Now I know very little of Holyoke, Mass., of my own knowledge. As a lecture-town I can say of it that its people are polite, but extremely undemonstrative, and that the lecturer is expected to furnish the refreshments. It is quite likely that the English lady was right, and that there are no foot-paths there.

I wish to say, however, that I know the

English lady. I know her—many, many of her—and I have met her a-many times. I know the enchanted fairyland in which her wistful memory loves to linger. Often and often have I watched her father's wardian-case grow into " papa's hot-houses;" the plain brick house that he leases, out Notting Hill way, swell into " our family mansion," and the cottage that her family once occupied at Stoke Wigglesworth change itself into " the country place that papa had to give up because it took so much of his time to see that it was properly kept up." And long experience in this direction enables me to take that little remark about the foot-paths, and to derive from it a large amount of knowledge about Holyoke and its surroundings that I should not have had of my own getting, for I have never seen Holyoke except by night, nor am I like to see it again.

From that brief remark I know these things about Holyoke: It is surrounded by a beautiful country, with rolling hills and a generally diversified landscape. There are beautiful green fields, I am sure. There is a fine river somewhere about, and I think there must be water-falls and a pretty little creek. The timber must be very fine, and probably there are some superb New England elms. The roads must be good, uncommonly good; and there must be unusual facilities for getting around and picnicking and finding charming views and all that sort of thing.

Nor does it require much art to learn all this from that pathetic plaint about the foot-paths. For the game of the Briton in a foreign land is ever the same. It changes not from generation unto generation. Bid him to the feast and set before him all your wealth of cellar and garner. Spread before him the meat, heap up for him the fruits of the season. Weigh down the board with every vegetable that the gardener's art can bring to perfection in or out of its time—white-potatoes, sweet-potatoes, lima-beans, string-beans, fresh peas, sweet-corn, lettuce, cauliflower, Brussels sprouts, tomatoes, musk-melons and water-melons—all you will—no word will you hear from him till he has looked over the whole assortment and discovered that you have not the vegetable

marrow, and that you do not raise it. Then
will he break forth and cry out for his vegetable marrow. All these things are naught to
him if he cannot have his vegetable marrow,
and he will tell you about the exceeding good-
ness and rarity of the vegetable marrow, until
you will figure it in your mind like unto the
famous mangosteen fruit of the Malay Penin-
sula, he who once eats whereof tastes never
again any other fruit of the earth, finding them
all as dust and ashes by the side of the mangosteen.

That is to say, this will happen unless you
have eaten of the vegetable marrow, and have
the presence of mind to recall to the Briton's
memory the fact that it is nothing but a sec-
ond-choice summer squash; after which the
meal will proceed in silence. Just so might
Mr. Burroughs have brought about a sudden
change in the topic of conversation by telling
the English lady that where the American
treads out a path he builds a road by the side
of it.

To tell the truth, I think that the English
foot-path is something pathetic beyond de-

scription. The better it is, the older, the better worn, the more it speaks with a sad significance of the long established inequalities of old-world society. It means too often the one poor, pitiful right of a poor man, the man who must walk all his life, to go hither and thither through the rich man's country. The lady may walk it for pleasure if she likes, but the man who walks it because he must, turns up a little by-path leading from it to a cottage that no industry or thrift will make his own; and for him to aspire to a roadway to his front-door would be a gross piece of impertinence in a man of his station. It is the remembrance of just such right-of-way foot-paths as the English lady's sad heart yearned after that reconciles me to a great many hundreds of houses that have recently been built in the State of New Jersey after designs out of books that cost all the way from twenty-five cents to a dollar. Architecturally these are very much inferior to the English cottager's home, and they occasionally waken thoughts of incendiarism. But the people who live in them are people who insist on having roads right to their front-doors, and I have heard them do some mighty interesting talking in town-meeting about the way those roads shall be laid and who shall do the laying.

As I have before remarked, I am quite willing to believe that Holyoke is a pathless wilderness, in the English lady's sense. But when Mr. Burroughs makes the generalization that there are no foot-paths in this country, it seems to me he must be letting his boyhood get too far away from him.

For there are foot-paths enough, certainly. Of course an old foot-path in this country always serves to mark the line of a new road when the people who had worn it take to keeping horses. But there are thousands of miles of paths criss-crossing the country-side in all of our older States that will never see the dirt-cart or the stone-crusher in the lifetime of any man alive to-day.

Mr. Burroughs—especially when he is published in the dainty little Douglas duodecimos—is one of the authors whose books a busy man reserves for a pocket-luxury of travel. So it was that, a belated reader, I came across

" THROUGH THE RICH MAN'S COUNTRY "

his lament over our pathlessness, some years after my having had a hand—or a foot, as you might say—in the making of a certain cross-lots foot-way which led me to study the windings and turnings of the longer country-side walks until I got the idea of writing " The Story of a Path." I am sorry to contradict Mr. Burroughs, but, if there are no foot-paths in America, what becomes of the many good golden hours that I have spent in well-tracked woodland ways and in narrow foot-lanes through the wind-swept meadow grass ? I cannot give these up; I can only wish that Mr. Burroughs had been my companion in them.

A foot-path is the most human thing in inanimate nature. Even as the print of his thumb reveals the old offender to the detectives, so the path tells you the sort of feet that wore it. Like the human nature that created it, it starts out to go straight when strength and determination shape its course, and it goes crooked when weakness lays it out. Until you begin to study them you can have no notion of the differences of character that exist among foot-paths. One line of trodden earth seems to you the same as another. But look! Is the path you are walking on fairly straight from point to point, yet deflected to avoid short rises and falls, *and is it worn to grade?* That is, does it plough a deep way through little humps and hillocks something as a street is cut down to grade? If you see this path before you, you may be sure that it is made by the heavy shuffle of workingmen's feet. A path that wavers from side to side, especially if the turns be from one bush to another, and that is only a light trail making an even line of wear over the inequalities of the ground—that is a path that children make. The path made by the business man—the man who is anxious to get to his work at one end of the day, and anxious to get to his home at the other—is generally a good piece of engineering. This type of man makes more paths in this country than he does in any other. He carries his intelligence and his energy into every act of life, and even in the half-unconscious business of making his own private trail he generally manages to find the line of least resistance in getting from one given point to another.

This is the story of a path:

It is called Reub Levi's Path, because Reuben Levi Dodd is supposed to have made it, some time in 1830 or thereabout, when he built his house on the hill. But it is much older than Reuben Levi. He probably thought he was telling the truth when, forty years ago, he swore to having broken the path himself twenty years before, through the Jacobus woods, down the hill and across the flat lands that then belonged to the Onderdoncks, and again through the Ogden woods to the county road; but he forgot that on the bright June day when he first started to find a convenient way through the woods and over the broad lowland fields from his own front-door to that of his father-in-law, Evert Ogden, and then through Mr. Ogden's patch of woods to the little town on the bank of the Passaic—he forgot that for a little part of the way he had had the help of a man whose feet had long before done with walking the paths of earth.

The forest, for it was a forest then, was full of heavy underwood and brush, and he had no choice but to dodge his way between the clumps. But when he got out to the broad open space on the brow of the hill, where no trees had ever grown, he found an almost

tropical growth of wild grass and azalea, with bull-brier twining over everything in every direction. He found it worse than the dense woods.

" Drat the pesky stuff," he said to himself;
" ain't there no way through it ?" Then as he
looked about he spied a line no broader than
his hand at the bottom, that opened clean
through the bull-brier and the bushes across
the open to where the trees began again on
the down-slope of the hill. Grass was growing in it, but he knew it for an old trail.

" 'Twas Pelatiah Jinks made that, I'll bet a
shilling," he said to himself, remembering the
lonely old trapper who had dwelt on that
mountain in his father's time. He had once
seen old man Jinks's powder-horn, with its
elaborate carving, done in the long solitary
hours when the old man sat weather-bound in
his lofty hermitage.

" Jest like the old critter to make a bee-line
track like that. But what in thunder did he
want to go that way across the clearing for ?
I'm much obleeged to him for his trail, but it
ain't headed right for town."

No, it was not. But young Dodd did not
remember that the trees whose tops he saw
just peeping over the hill were young things
of forty years' growth that had taken the

8

place of a line of ninety-year-old chestnuts
that had died down from the top and been
broken down by the wind shortly after old

Pelatiah died. The line that the old man had
made for himself took him straight to the one
little hillock where he could look over this tall

screen and get his bearings afresh by the glint
of the Passaic's water in the woody valley
below, for at no other spot along that ridge
was the Passaic visible.

Now in this one act of Reuben Levi Dodd
you can see the human nature that lies at the
bottom of all path-making. He turned aside
from his straight course to walk in the easy
way made by another man, and then fetched a
compass, as they used to say in the Apostle
Paul's time, to get back to his straight bearings. Old Pelatiah had a good reason for
deviating from his straight line to the town;
young Dodd had none, except that it was
wiser to go two yards around than to go one
yard straight through the bull-brier. Young
Dodd had a powder-horn slung from his shoulder that morning, and the powder-horn had
some carving on it, but it was not like the
carving on old Pelatiah's horn. There was a
letter R, cut with many flourishes, a letter L
cut but wanting most of its flourishes, and a
letter D half finished, and crooked at that, and
without the first trace of a flourish. That
was the way his powder-horn looked that

day, for that was the way it looked when he died, and his son sold it to a dealer in antiquities.

Young Dodd and his wife found it lonely living up there on the hill-top. They were the first who had pushed so far back from the river and the town. Mrs. Dodd, who had an active and ambitious spirit in her, often reproached her husband for his neglect to make their home more accessible to her old friends in the distant town.

" If you'd take a bill-hook," she would say, " and clean up that snake-fence path of yours a little, may be folks would climb up here to see us once in a blue moon. It's all well enough for you with your breeches, but how are women folks to trail their frocks through that brush ? "

Reub Levi would promise and promise, and once he did take his hook and chop out a hundred yards or so. But things did not mend until Big Bill Turnbull, known all over the county as the Hard Job Man, married a widow with five children, bought a little patch of five or six acres next to Dodd's big farm, built a log-cabin for himself and his family, and settled down there.

Now Turnbull's log-cabin was so situated that the line of old Pelatiah's path through the bull-brier, extended about an eighth of a mile, would just reach the front-door.   Turnbull saw this, and it was at that point that he tapped Reub Levi's foot-path to the town. But he did his tapping after his own fashion. He took his wife's red flannel petticoat and tied it to a sapling on the top of the mound that the old hunter used to climb, and then with bill-hook and axe he cut a straight swath through the woods.   He even cut down through the roots and took out the larger stones.

"That's what you'd ought to have done long ago, Reuben Levi Dodd," said his wife, as she watched this manifestation of energy.

"Guess I didn't lose much by waiting," Reub Levi answered, with a smile that did not look as self-satisfied as he tried to make it. "I'd a-had to do it myself, and now the other fellow's done it for me."

And thereafter he took Bill Turnbull's path just where it touched the corner of his own

cleared land.   But Malvina Dodd, to the day
of her death, never once walked that way, but,

going and coming, took the winding track that
her husband had laid out for her when their
home was built.

The next maker of the path was a boy not ten years old. His name was Philip Wessler, and he was a charity boy of German parentage, who had been adopted by an eccentric old man in the town, an herb-doctor. This calling was in more repute in those days than it is now. Old Doctor Van Wagener was growing feeble, and he relied on the boy, who was grateful and faithful, to search for his stock of simples. When the weather was favorable they would go together through the Ogden woods, and across the meadows to where the other woods began at the bottom of the hill. Here the old man would sit down and wait, while the boy climbed the steep hillside, and ranged hither and thither in his search for sassafras and liverwort, and a hundred and one plants, flowers, and herbs, in which the doctor found virtue. When he had collected his bundle he came running down the path to where the doctor sat, and left them for the old man to pick and choose from, while he darted off after another load.

He did a boy's work with the path. Steep grades were only a delight to him, and so in the course of a year or two he trod out, or jumped out, a series of break-neck short-cuts. William Turnbull—people called him William

now, since he had built a clap-board house, and was using the log-cabin for a barn—William Turnbull, observing these short-cuts, approved of their purpose, but not of their method. He went through the woods once or twice on odd days after his hay was in, and did a little grading with a mattock. Here and there he made steps out of flat stones. He told his wife he thought it would be some

handier for her, and she told him—they were both from Connecticut — that it was quite some handier, and that it was real thoughtful of him; and that she didn't want to speak no ill of the dead, but if her first man had been that considerate he wouldn't never have got himself drowned going pickerel fishing in March, when the ice was so soft you'd suppose rational folks would keep off of it.

This path was a path of slow formation. It was a path that was never destined to become a road. It is only in mathematics that a straight line is the shortest distance between two points. The grade through the Jacobus woods was so steep that no wagon could have been hauled up it over the mud roads of that day and generation. Lumber, groceries, and all heavy truck were taken around by the road, that made a clean sweep around the hill, and was connected with the Dodd and Turnbull farms by a steep but short lane which the workmen had made when they built the Dodd house. The road was six miles to the path's three, but the drive was shorter than the walk.

There was a time when it looked as though the path might really develop into a road. That was the time when the township, having outgrown the county roads, began to build roads for itself. But, curiously enough, two subjects of Great Britain settled the fate of that New Jersey path. The controversy between Telford and Macadam was settled so long ago in Macadam's favor, that few remember the point of difference between those two noted engineers. Briefly stated, it was this: Mr. Telford said it *was*, and Mr. Macadam said it was *not*, necessary to put a foundation of large flat stones, set on end, under a broken-stone road. Reuben Levi's township, like many other New Jersey townships, sided with Mr. Telford, and made a mistake that cost thousands of dollars directly, and millions indirectly. To-day New Jersey can show the way to all her sister States in road-building and road-keeping. But the money she wasted on costly Telford pavements is only just beginning to come back to her, as she spreads out mile after mile of the economical Macadam. Reuben Levi's township squandered money on a few miles of Telford, raised the tax-rate higher than it had ever been before, and opened not one inch of new road for fifteen years thereafter. And within that fifteen years the canal came up on one side, opening a way to the great manufacturing town, ten miles down the river; and then the town at the end of the path was no longer the sole base of supplies. Then the railroad came around on the other side of the hill, and put a flag-station just at the bottom of what had come to be known as Dodd's Lane. And thus by the magic of nineteenth-century science New York and Newark were brought nearer to the hillside farm than the town three miles away.

But year by year new feet trod the path. The laborers who cut the canal found it and took it when they left their shanty camp to go to town for Saturday-night frolics. Then William Turnbull, who had enlarged his own farm as far as he found it paid, took to buying land and building houses in the valley beyond. Reub Levi laughed at him, but he prospered after a way he had, and built up a thriving little settlement just over the canal. The people of this little settlement soon made a path that connected with Reuben Levi's, by way of William Turnbull's, and whenever business or old association took them to town

"THE LABORERS . . . FOUND IT AND TOOK IT"

they helped to make the path longer and broader.

By and by the regular wayfarers found it out —the peddlers, the colporteurs, the wandering portrait-painters, the tinkers and clock-menders, the runaway apprentices, and all the rest of the old-time gentry of the road. And they carried the path on still farther—down the river to Newark.

It is not wholly to be told, " The Story of the Path." So many people had to do with its making in so many ways that no chronicle could tell all the meanings of its twists and turns and straight lines. There is one little jog in its course to-day, where it went around a tree, the stump of which rotted down into the ground a quarter of a century ago. Why do we walk around that useless bend to-day ? Because it is a path, and because we walk in the way of human nature.

The life of a tree may be a hundred years or two hundred years and yet be long life. But the days of the age of a man are threescore and ten, and though some be so strong that they come to fourscore, yet the strong man

may be stricken down in the flower of his
strength, if it be the will of the Lord.

When William Turnbull came to die he was

but twoscore years and five, but for all he was
so young the people of the township gathered
from far and near, for he had been a helpful
man all his days, and those whom he had

helped remembered that he would help them no more. Four men and four women sat up with the dead, twice as many as the old custom called for. One of the men was a Judge, two had been Chosen Freeholders, and the fourth was his hired man. There was no cemetery in the township, and his tomb had been built at the bottom of the hill, looking out on the meadows which he had just made his own—the last purchase of his life.

There were two other pall-bearers to carry him on their shoulders to the place beyond which no man goes. These two, when they left the house on the night before the funeral, walked slowly and thoughtfully down the path together. They looked over every step of the way with to-morrow's slow and toilsome march in their minds. When they came to the turn by Pelatiah's mound they paused.

" We can't never get him round that bend," said one. " That ain't no way to start down the hill. Best is I come here first thing in the morning and cut a way through this bull-brier straight across the angle, then we can see ahead where we're going. Put them two light

9

men behind, and you and me at the head, and we can manage it. My! what a man *he* was, though! Why, I seen him take the head of a coffin all by himself once."

This man was a near neighbor of the Turnbulls, for now they had a number of neighbors; Reuben Levi Dodd had been selling small farms off his big farm—somehow he had never made the big farm a success. There are many services of men to man that country neighbors make little of, though to the dwellers in great cities they might seem strange burdens. At five o'clock the next morning Warren Freeman, the pall-bearer, went out and mowed and hacked a path through the tangled field from midway of old Pelatiah's trail down to a short-cut made by the doctor's charity boy, who was to-day a Judge. This Judge came out of the silent house, released by the waking hour, from his vigil with the dead. He watched his fellow pall-bearer at work.

"I used to go down that path on the dead run twenty years ago," said he, "when I was working for Dr. Van Wagener and he used to send me up here gathering herbs."

"I USED TO GO DOWN THAT PATH ON THE DEAD RUN"

" You'll go down it on the dead walk to-morrow, Jedge," said the other, pausing in his work, " and you want to step mighty careful, or one fun'l will breed another."

Life, death, wedlock, the lingering of lovers, the waywardness of childish feet, the tread of weary toil, the slow, swaying walk of the mother, with her babe in her arms, the meas-ured steps of the bearer of the dead, the light march of youth and strength and health—all, all have helped to beat out the strange, wan-dering line of the old path; and to me, who love to find and to tread its turns, the current of their human life flows still along its course, in the dim spaces under the trees, or out where the sunshine and the wind are at play upon the broad, bright meadows.

THE LOST CHILD

THE LOST CHILD

THE best of life in a great city is that it breeds a broad and tolerant catholicity of spirit: the best of country life is that it breeds the spirit of helpful, homely, kindly neighborliness. The suburban-dweller, who shares in both lives, is perhaps a little too ready to pride himself in having learned the lesson of the great metropolis, but the other and homelier lesson is taught so gradually and so unobtrusively, that he often learns it quite unconsciously; and goes back, perhaps, to his old existence in the city, only to realize that a certain charm has gone out of life which he misses without knowing just what he has lost. He thinks, perhaps, it is exercise he lacks. And it is, indeed—the exercise of certain gentle sympathies, that thrive as poorly in the

town's crowded life as the country wild-flowers
thrive in the flower-pots of tenement-house
windows.

It was between three and four o'clock of an
August night—a dark, warm, hazy night,
breathless, heavy and full of the smell of grass
and trees and dew-moistened earth, when a
man galloped up one of those long suburban
streets, where the houses stand at wide inter-
vals, each behind its trim lawn, or old-fashioned flower-garden, relieved, even in the
darkness, against a great rear-wood screen of
lofty trees.   Up the driveway of one of these
he turned, his horse's hoof-beats dropping
clear and sharp on the hard macadam.   He
reined up at the house and rapped a loud
tattoo with the stock of his whip on a pillar
of the veranda.

It was a minute or two before the noise,
loud as it was, had reached the ears of two
sleepers in the bedroom, just above his head.
A much less startling sound would have awakened a whole city household; but slumber in
the country has a slumber of its own : in summer time a slumber born of night-air, laden

with the odors of vegetation, and silent except
for the drowsy chirp of birds that stir in vine
and tree. The wife awoke first, listened for a
second, and aroused her husband, who went
to the window. He raised the screen and
looked out.

"Who is it?" he said, without nervousness
or surprise, though ten years before in his

city home such a summons might have shaken
his spirit with anxious dread.

"I'm Latimer," said the man on the horse,

briefly. " That boy of Penrhyn's—the little one with the yellow hair—is lost. He got up and slipped out the house, somehow, about an hour ago, they think, and they've found one of his playthings nearly half a mile down the Romneytown Road."

" Where shall I meet you ?" asked the man at the window.

" At the Gun-Club grounds on the hill," replied Latimer; " we've sent a barrel of oil up there for the lanterns. So long, Halford. Is Dirck at home ?"

" Yes," said Halford; and without another word Latimer galloped into the darkness, and in a minute the sound of his tattoo was heard on the hollow pillars of the veranda of the house next door.

This was the summons—a bare announcement of an event without appeal, request, suggestion, or advice. None of these things was needed. Enough had been said between the two men, though they knew each other only as distant neighbors. Each knew well what that summons meant, and what duty it involved.

The rat-tat of Latimer's crop had hardly

sounded before a cheery young voice rang out on the air.

" All right, old man ! I heard you at Halford's. Go ahead."

It was Dirck's voice. Dirck had another name, a good long, Holland-Dutch one, but everybody, even the children, called him by his Christian name, and as he had lived to thirty without getting one day older than eighteen, we will consider the other Dutch name unnecessary. Dirck and Halford were close friends and close neighbors. They were two men who had reached a point of perfect community of tastes and inclinations, though they came together in two widely different starting-places—though they were so little alike to outward seeming that they were known among their friends as " the mismates." Though one was forty and the other but thirty, each had closed a career, and was somewhat idly seeking a new one. As Dirck expressed it, " We two fellows had played our games out, and were waiting till we strike another that was high enough for our style. We ain't playing limit games."

Two very different games they had been, but neither had been a small one. Dirck had started in with a fortune to " do " the world— the whole world, nothing else would suit him. He had been all over the globe. He had lived among all manner of peoples. He had ridden everything ridable, shot everything shootable, climbed everything climbable, and satisfied himself, as he said, that the world was too small for any particular use. At the end of his travels he had a little of his fortune left, a vast amount of experience, the constitution of a red Indian, and a vocabulary so vast and so peculiar that it stunned and fascinated the stranger. Halford was a New York lawyer, gray, clean-shaven, and sharp of feature. His " game " had made him famous and might have made him wealthy, but he cared neither for fame nor wealth. For twenty years he had fought a host of great corporations to establish one single point of law. His antagonists had vainly tried to bribe him, and as vainly to bully him. He had been assaulted, his life had been threatened, and altogether, as he admitted, the game had been lively enough to keep him interested; but having once won the game he tired of that style of play altogether. He picked out a small but choice

practice which permitted him to work or be idle pretty much as the fancy took him. These were two odd chums to meet in a small suburban town, there to lead quiet and uneventful lives, and yet they were the two most contented men in the place.

Halford was getting into his clothes, but really with a speed and precision which got the job over before his impetuous next-door neighbor had got one leg of his riding-breeches on. Mrs. Halford sat up in bed and expressed her feeling to her husband, who had never been known to express his.

"Oh, Jack," she said, "isn't it awful? Would you ever have thought of such a thing! They must have been awfully careless! Oh, Jack, you will find him, won't you? Jack, if such a thing happened to one of our children I should go wild; I'll never get over it myself if he isn't found. Oh, you don't know how thankful I am that we didn't lose our Richard that way! Oh, Jack, dear, isn't it too horrible for anything!"

Jack simply responded, with no trace of emotion in his voice:

"It's the hell!"

And yet in those three words Jack Halford expressed, in his own way, quite as much as his wife had expressed in hers. More, even, for there was a grim promise in his tone that comforted her heart.

Mrs. Halford's feelings being expressed and in some measure relieved, she promptly became practical.

"I'll fill your flask, of course, dear. Brandy, I suppose? And what shall we women take up to the Gun Club besides blankets and clean clothes?"

Mrs. Halford's husband always thought before he spoke, and she was not at all surprised that he filled his tobacco-pouch before he answered. When he did speak he knew what he had to say.

" First something to put in my pocket for Dirck and me to eat. We can't fool with coming home to breakfast. Second, tell the girls to send up milk to the Gun Club, and something for you women to eat."

" Oh, I sha'n't want anything to eat," cried Mrs. Halford.

" You must eat," said her husband, simply, " and you must make the rest of them eat. You might do all right without it, but I wouldn't trust the rest of them. You may need all the nerve you've got."

" Yes, dear," said his wife, submissively. She had been with her husband in times of danger, and she knew he was a leader to be followed. " I'll have sandwiches and coffee and tea; I can make them drink tea, anyway."

" Third," went on Jack Halford, as if he had not been interrupted, " bring my field-glass with you. Dirck and I will range together along the river. If I put up a white handkerchief anywhere down there, you stay where you are and we will come to you. If I put up this red one, come right down with blankets and brandy in the first carriage you can get hold of. Get on the north edge of the hill and you can keep a line on us almost anywhere."

" Couldn't you give us some signal, dear, to tell us if—if—if it's all right ? "

" If it was all wrong," replied the husband, " you wouldn't want the mother to learn it that way. I'll signal to you privately, however. If it's all right, I'll wave the handkerchief; if I move it up and down, you'll understand."

Two minutes later he bade her good-by at the door.

" Now remember," he said, " white means wait, red means ride."

And having delivered himself of this simple mnemonic device, he passed out into the darkness.

At the next gate he met Dirck and the two swung into step together, and walked up the street with the steady stretching tread of men accustomed to walking long distances. They said " Hello! " as they met, and their further conversation was brief.

" River," said Halford; " what do you think ?"

" River, sure," said the other; " a lot of those younger boys have been taking the youngsters down there lately. I saw that kid down there last week, and I'll bet a dollar his mother would swear that he'd never seen the river."

" Then we won't say anything about it to her," said Halford, and they reached along in silence.

Before them, when they came to the end of the road, rose a hill with a broad plateau on its stomach. Here through the dull haze of the morning they saw smoky-orange lights beginning to flicker uncertainly as the wind that heralds the sunrise came fitfully up. The soft wet grass under their feet was flecked with little grayish-silver cobwebs, and here and there they heard the morning chirp of ground-nesting birds. As they went farther up the hill a hum of voices came from above; the voices of people, men and women, mingled and consonant like the voices of the birds, but with a certain tone of trouble and expectancy. Every now and then one individual voice or another would dominate the general murmur, and would be followed by a quick flutter of sound denoting acquiescence or disagreement. From this they knew that most of their neighbors had arrived before them, having been summoned earlier in the journey of the messengers sent out from the distant home of the lost child.

On the crown of the hill stood a curious structure, actually small, but looming large in the grayness. The main body of the building was elevated upon posts, and was smaller at the bottom than where the spreading walls met the peaked roof. This roof spread out on both sides into broad verandas, and under these two wing-like shelters some three or four score of people were clustered in little groups. Lanterns and hand-lamps dimly lit up faces that showed strange in the unfamiliar illumination. There were women with shawls over their shoulders and women with shawls

over their heads. Some of the men were in
their shirt-sleeves, some wore shooting-coats,

and a few had overcoats, though the night was
warm. But no stranger arriving on the scene
could have taken it for a promiscuous or acci-

dental assemblage.   There was a movement in unison, a sympathetic stir throughout the little crowd that created a common interest and a common purpose.   The arrival of the two men was hailed with that curious sound with which such a gathering greets a desired and attended accession—not quite the sigh of relief, but the quick, nervous expulsion of the breath that tallies the coming of the expected.   These were two of the men to be counted on, and they were there.

Every little community such as this knows its leaders, and now that their number was complete, the women drew together by themselves save for two or three who clearly took equal direction with the men ; and a dozen in all, perhaps, gathered in a rough circle to discuss the organization of the search.

It was a brief discussion.   A majority of the members of the group had formed decided opinions as to the course taken by the wandering child, and thus a division into sub-groups came about at once.   This left various stretchings of territory uncovered, and these were assigned to those of the more decided minority who were best acquainted with the particular localities. When the division of labor was completed, the men had arranged to start out in such directions as would enable them to range and view the whole countryside for the extreme distance of radius to which it was supposed the boy could possibly have travelled. The assignment of Halford and Dirck to the river course was prompt, for it was known that they habitually hunted and fished along that line. The father of the boy, who stood by, was reminded of this fact, for a curious and doubtful look came into his face when he heard two of the most active and energetic men in the town set aside to search a region where he had no idea that his boy could have strayed. Some excuse was given also for the detailing of two other men of equal ability to take the range immediately above the river bank, and within hailing distance of those in the marshes by the shore. Had his mind not been in the daze of mortal grief and perplexity, he would have grasped the sinister significance of this precaution; but he accepted it in dull and hopeless confidence. When after they

had set forth he told his wife of the arrange-
ments made, and she heard the names of the
four men who had been appointed to work
near the riverside, she pulled the faded old

Paisley shawl (that the
child's nurse had
wrapped about her)
across her swollen eyes,
and moaned, "The river,
the river—oh, my boy,
my boy!"

Perhaps the men heard
her, for being all in
place to take their several directions, they
made a certain broken start and were off into
the darkness at the base of the hill, before the
two or three of their sex who were left in
charge of the women had fairly given the
word. The tramp of men's feet and horses'
hoofs died down into the shadowy distance.
The women went inside the spacious old corn-
crib that had been turned into a gun-club
shooting-box, and there the mother laid her
face on the breast of her best friend, and clung
to her without a sound, only shuddering once

and again, and holding her with a convulsive grip. The other women moved around, and busied themselves with little offices, like the making of tea and the trimming of lamps, and talked among each other in a quiet way with the odd little upward inflections with which women simulate cheerfulness and hope, telling tales of children who had been lost and had been found again all safe and unscathed, and praising the sagacity and persistence of certain of the men engaged in the search. Mr. Latimer, they said, was almost like a detective, he had such an instinct for finding things and people. Mr. Brown knew every field and hollow on the Brookfield Road. Mr. MacDonald could see just as well in the darkness as in the daytime; and all the talk that reached the mother's ears was of this man's skill of woodcraft, of that man's knowledge of the country, or of another's unfailing cleverness or tirelessness.

Outside, the two or three men in charge stood by the father in their own way. It had been agreed that he should wait at the hilltop to learn if a trail had been found. He was a good fellow, but not helpful or capable; and it was their work to "jolly" him, as they called it; to keep his hope up with cheering suggestions, and with occasional judicious doses of whiskey from their flasks. For themselves, they did not drink; though their voices were low and steady they were more nervous than the poor sufferer they guarded, numbed and childish in his awful grief and apprehension. They were waiting for the sounds of the beginning of the search far below, and presently these sounds came, or rather one sound, a hollow noise, changeful, uneven, yet of a cruel monotony. It was a cry of "Willy! Willy! Willy!" rising out of that gray-black depth, a cry of many voices, a cry that came from far and near, a cry at which the women huddled closer together and pressed each other's hands, and looked speechless love and pity at the woman who lay upon her best friend's breast, clutching it tighter and tighter. Of the men outside, the father leaned forward and clutched the arm of his chair. The others saw the great drops of sweat roll from his brow, and they turned their faces away from him and swore inaudibly.

Then, as the deep below began to be alive
with a faint dim light reflected from the half
awakened heaven, the voices died away in the
distance, and in their place the leaves of the

great trees rustled and the birds twittered to
the coming morn.

   .   .   .   .

The day broke with the dull red that prophe-
sies heat. As the hours wore on the prophecy
was fulfilled. The moisture of the dew and

the river mist rose toward the hot sky and vanished, but the dry haze remained and the low sun shone through it with a peculiar diffusion of coppery light. Even when it reached the zenith, the warm, faintly yellow dimness still rose high above the horizon, throwing its soft spell upon all objects far or near, and melting through the dim blue on the distant hilltop into the hot azure of the great dome above.

For an hour the watchers on the hill remained undisturbed, talking in undertones. For the most part, they speculated on the significance of the faint sounds that came up from below. Sometimes they could trace the crash of a horse through dry underbrush; sometimes a tumultuous clamor of commanding voices would tell them that a flat boat was being worked across a broad creek or a pond; sometimes a hardly audible whirr, and the metallic clinking of a bicycle bell would tell them that the wheelmen were speeding on the search. But for the best part of the time only nature's harmony of sounds came up through the ever-lightening gloom.

But with the first of daylight came the neighbors who had not been summoned, and they, of course, came running. It was also noticeable of this contingent that their attire was somewhat studied, and showed more or less elaborate preparation for starting on the already started hunt. Noticeable also it was, that after much sagacious questioning and profoundly wise discussion, the most of the newcomers either hung about peering out into the dawn and making startling discoveries at various points, or else went back to their houses to get bicycles, or horses, or forgotten suspenders. The little world of a suburban town sorts itself out pretty quickly and pretty surely. There are the men who do and the men who don't; and very few of the men who *did*, in that particular town, were in bed half an hour after the loss of that child was known.

But, after all, the late arrivals were useful in their way, and their wives, who came along later, were still more useful. The men were fertile in suggestions for tempting and practicable breakfasts; and the women actually brought the food along; and by the time that the world was well alight, the early risers were bustling about and serving coffee and tea, and biscuits and fruit, and keeping up that semblance of activity and employment that alone can carry poor humanity through long periods of suspense and anxiety. And the first on the field were the last to eat and the least critical of their fare.

It was eight o'clock when the first party of searchers returned to the hill. There were eight of them. They stopped a little below the crib and beckoned to Penrhyn to come down to them. He went, white-faced and a little unsteady on his feet; his guardians followed him and joined with the group in a busy serious talk that lasted perhaps five minutes—but vastly longer to the women who watched them from above. Then Penrhyn and two men went hastily down the hill, and the others came up to the crib and eagerly accepted the offer of a hasty breakfast.

They had little to tell, and that little only served to deepen the doubt and trouble of the hour. Of all the complication of unkind chance the searchers had to face the worst and

the most puzzling. As in many towns of old
settlement a road ran around the town, roughly
circumscribing it, much as the boulevards of
Paris anciently circumscribed the old fortifi-
cations of the city. It was little more than
a haphazard connection of roads, lanes, and
avenues, each one of which had come into
existence to serve some particular end, and
the connection had ended in forming a circuit
that practically defined the town limits. It
had been made certain that the boy had wandered this whole round, and that he had not
left it by any one of the converging roads
which he must have crossed. Nor could the
direction of his wandering be ascertained. The
hard, dry macadam road, washed clean by a
recent rainfall, showed no trace of his light,
infantile footprints. But sure it was that he
had been on the road not one hour, but two
or three at least, and that he had started out
with an armful of his tiny belongings. Here
they had found his small pocket-handkerchief,
there a gray giraffe from his Noah's ark; in
another place a noseless doll that had de-
scended to him from his eldest sister; then a

top had been found—a top that he could not have spun for years to come. Would the years ever come when that lost boy should spin tops?

There were other little signs which attested his passage around the circle—freshly broken stalks of milkweed, shreds of his brightly fig-ured cotton dress on the thorns of the wayside blackberries, and even in one place the clear print of a muddy and bloody little hand on a white gate-post.

There is no search more difficult than a search for a lost child five or six years of age. We are apt to think of these wee ones as feeble creatures, and we forget that their physical strength is proportionally much greater than that of grown-up people. We forget also that the child has not learned to attribute sensations of physical discomfort to their proper sources. The child knows that it suffers, but it does not know why. It is con-scious of a something wrong, but the little brain is often unable to tell whether that something be weariness or hunger. If the wandering spirit be upon it, it wanders to the last limit of physical power, and it is surprising indeed to find how long it is before that limit is reached. A healthy, muscular infant of this age has been known to walk nearly eight or ten miles before becoming utterly exhausted. And when exhaustion comes, and the tiny form falls in its tracks, how small an object it is to detect in the great world of outdoors! A little bundle of dusty garments in a ditch, in a wayside hollow, in tall grass, or among the tufts and hummocks of a marsh —how easy it is for so inconspicuous an object to escape the eye of the most zealous searcher! A young animal lost cries incessantly; the lost child cries out his pitiful little cry, finds itself lifted to no tender bosom, soothed by no gentle voice, and in the end wanders and suffers in helpless, hopeless silence.

As the morning wore on Dirck and Halford beat the swampy lands of the river-side with a thoroughness that showed their understanding of the difficulty of their work, and their conviction that the child had taken that direction. This conviction deepened with every hour, for the rest of the countryside was fairly open and

well populated, and there the search should
have been, for such a search, comparatively
easy. Yet the sun climbed higher and higher
in the sky, and no sound of guns fired in glad
signal reached their ears. Hither and thither
they went through the hot lowlands, meeting
and parting again, with appointments to come
together in spots known to them both, or
separating without a word, each knowing well
where their courses would bring them together.
From time to time they caught glimpses of
their companions on the hills above, who, from
their height, could see the place of meeting on
the still higher hill, and each time they sig-
nalled the news and got back the despairing
sign that meant " None yet!"

News enough there was, but not *the* news.
Mrs. Penrhyn still stayed, for her own house
was so situated that the child could not possibly return to it, if he had taken the direction
that now seemed certain, without passing
through the crowd of searchers, and intelligence of his discovery must reach her soonest
at that point. Perhaps there was another reason, too. Perhaps she could not bear to

return to that silent house, where every room held some reminder of her loss. Certainly she remained at the Club, and perhaps she got some unreasoning comfort out of the rumors and reports that came to that spot from every side. It was but the idle talk that springs up and flies about on such occasions, but now and then it served as a straw for her drowning hope to clutch at. Word would come of a farmer who had seen a strange child in his neighbor's wagon. Then would come a story of an inn-keeper who had driven into town to ask if anybody had lost a boy. Then somebody would bring a report at third or fourth hand of a child rescued alive from the river. Of course story after story, report after report, came to nothing. The child seen in the wagon was a girl of fourteen. The inn-keeper had come to town to ask about the lost child, but it was only because he had heard the report and was curious. A child indeed had been rescued from the river, but the story was a week old. And so it went, and the hot sun rose to the zenith and declined, and the coppery haze grew dim, and the shadows lengthened, and the late afternoon was come with its awful threat of impending night.

Dirck and Halford, down in the riverside marsh, saw that dreaded change fall upon the

landscape, and they paused in their search and looked at one another silently. They had been ceaselessly at work all day, and the work had left its marks on them. Their faces were burnt to a fiery red, they were torn and scratched in the brambles, their clothes were soaked in mud and water to the waist, and they had been bitten and stung by insects until they looked as though some strange fever had broken out on them.

They had just met after a long beat, each having described the half of a circle around a piece of open water, and had sunk down in utter weariness on a little patch of dry ground, and for a minute looked at each other in silence. Then the younger man spoke.

" Hal," he said, " he never came this far."

By way of answer the other drew from his pocket a child's shoe, worn and wet, and held it up.

" Where did you find it ?" asked Dirck.

" Right over there," said Halford, " near that old wagon-trail."

Dirck looked at him with a question in his eyes, which found its answer in the grave inclination of the elder's head. Then Dirck shook his own head and whistled—one long, low, significant whistle.

" Well," he said, " I thought so. Any trail ?"

" Not the least," replied Halford. " There's a strip of thick salt grass there, over two yards wide, and I found the shoe right in the middle of it. It was lying on its side when I found it, not caught in the grass."

" Then they were carrying him, sure," said Dirck, decisively. " Now then, the question is, which way."

The two men went over to the abandoned roadway, a mere trail of ruts, where, in years before, ox-teams had hauled salt hay. Up and down the long strip of narrow grass that bordered it, they went backward and forward, hunting for traces of men's feet, for they knew by this time, almost beyond doubt, that the child was in the hands of tramps. The " tramp-hole " is an institution in all suburban regions which are bordered by stretches of wild and unfrequented country. These tramp-holes or camps are the headquarters of bands of wanderers who come year after year to dwell sometimes for a week, sometimes for months. The same spot is always occupied, and there seems to be an understanding among all the bands that the original territory shall not be exceeded. The tramps who establish these " holes " are invariably professionals, and never casual vagabonds; and apparently they make it a point of honor to conduct themselves with a certain propriety while they

are in camp. Curiously enough, too, they seem to come to the tramp-hole, mainly for the purpose of doing what it is supposed that a tramp never does, namely: washing themselves and their clothes. I have seen on a chill November day, in one of these places, half a dozen men, naked to the waist, scrubbing themselves, or drying their wet shirts before the fire. I have always found them perfectly peaceable, and I have never known them to accost lonely passers-by, or women or children. If a shooting or fishing party comes along, however, large enough to put any accusation of terrorism out of the question, it is not uncommon for the "hoboes" to make a polite suggestion that the poor man would be the better for his beer; and so well is the reputation of these queer camps established that the applicant generally receives such a collection of five-cent pieces as will enable him to get a few quarts for himself and his companions.

Still, in spite of the mysterious system of government that sways these banded wanderers on the face of the earth, it happens occasionally that the tramp of uncontrollable instincts finds his way into the tramp-hole, and there, if his companions are not numerous or strong enough to withstand him, commits some outrage that excites popular indignation and leads to the utter abolition of one of the few poor out-door homes that the tramp can call his own, by the grace and indulgence of the world of workers. That such a thing had happened now the two searchers for the lost child feared with an unspeakable fear.

Dirck straightened himself up after a careful inspection of the strip of salt grass turf, and looking up at the ridge, blew a loud, shrill whistle on his two fingers. There was no answer. They had gone a full mile beyond call of their followers.

" I'll tell you what, old man," said Dirck, with the light of battle coming into his young eyes, " we'll do this thing ourselves." His senior smiled, but even as he smiled he knit his brows.

" I'll go you, my boy," he said, " so far as to look them up at the canal-boats. If they are not there we've got to go back and start the rest off. It may be a question of horses, and it may be a question of telegraphing."

" Well, let's have one go at them, anyway," said Dirck. He was no less tender-hearted than his companion; he wanted to find the child, but also he wanted, being young and strong and full of fight, to hunt tramps.

There were three tramp-holes by the river-side, but two were sheltered hollows used only in the winter-time. The third was a collection of abandoned canal-boats on the muddy strand of the river. Most of them were hopeless wrecks; in three or four a few patches of deck remained, enough to afford lodgment and shelter to the reckless wayfarers who made nothing of sleeping close to the polluted waters that permeated the rotten hulks with foul stains and fouler smells.

From the largest of these long, clumsy carcasses of boats came a sound of muffled laughter. The two searchers crept softly up, climbed noiselessly to the deck and looked down the hatchway. The low, red sun poured in through a window below them, leaving them in shadow and making a picture in red light and black shades of the strange group below.

Surrounded by ten tramps; ten dirty, uncouth, unshaven men of the road, sat the little Penrhyn boy, his little night-shirt much travel-stained and torn, his fat legs scratched and bruised, his soiled cheeks showing the traces of tears, his lips dyed with the juices of the berries he had eaten on his way, but happy, happy, happy—happier perhaps than he had ever been in his life before; for in his hand he held a clay pipe which he made persistent efforts to smoke, while one of the men, a big black-bearded animal who wore three coats, one on top of the other, gently withdrew it from his lips each time that the smoke grew dangerously thick. And the whole ten of them, sitting around him in their rags and dirt, cheered him and petted him and praised him, even as no polite assemblage had ever worshipped him before. No food, no drink could have been so acceptable to that delicately nurtured child of the house of Penrhyn as the rough admiration of those ten tramps. Whatever terrors, sufferings, or privations he had been through were all forgotten, and he crowed and shrieked with hysterical laughter. And when his two rescuers dropped down into the hole, instead of welcoming them with joy, he grabbed one of the collars of the big brute with the three coats and wept in dire disappointment and affright.

" Fore God, boss!" said the spokesman of
the gang, the sweat standing out on his brow,
" we didn't mean him no harm, and we
wouldn't have done him no harm neither. We
found de little blokey over der in the ma'sh
yonder, and we tuk him in and fed him de
best we could. We was goin' to take him up
to the man what keeps the gin-mill up the river
there, for we hadn't no knowledge where he
come from, and we didn't want to get none of
you folks down on us. I know we oughter
have took him up two hours ago, but he was
foolin' that funny-like that we all got kinder
stuck on it, see, and we kinder didn't want to
shake him. That's all there was to it, boss.
God in heaven be my judge, I ain't lyin', and
that's the truth!"

The faces of the ten tramps could not turn
white, but they did show an ashen fear under
their eyes—a deadly fear of the two men for
whom any one of them would have been more
than a match, but who represented the world
from which they were outcasts, the world of
Home, of whose most precious sweetness they
had stolen an hour's enjoyment—the world so

strong and terrible to avenge a wrong to its best beloved.

Then the silence was broken by the voice of the child, wailing piteously:

" I don't want to be tooken away from the raggedty gentlemen!"

Dirck still looked suspicious as he took the

weeping child, but Halford smiled grimly, thoughtfully and sadly, as he put his hand in his pocket and said: " I guess it's all right, boys, but I think you'd better get away for the present. Take this and get over the river and out of the county. The people have been searching for this baby all day, and I don't know whether they'll listen to my friend and me."

.   .   .   .

The level red light had left the valleys and low places, and lit alone the hilltop where the mother was watching, when a great shout came out of the darkness, spreading from voice to voice through the great expanse below, and echoed wildly from above, thrilling men's blood and making hearts stand still; and as it rose and swelled and grew toward her out of the darkness, the mother knew that her lost child was found.

A LETTER TO TOWN

A LETTER TO TOWN

FERNSEED STATION,
ATLANTIS CO., NEW ——
February 30, 189-.

M Y DEAR MODESTUS:—You write
me that circumstances have decided
you to move your household from New York
to some inexpensively pleasant town, village,
or hamlet in the immediate neighborhood, and
you ask me the old, old innocent question:

" Shall I like suburban life ? "

This question I can answer most frankly and
positively:

" No, certainly not.   You will not like it at
all."

There is no such thing as *liking* a country
life—for I take it that you mean to remove to
the real suburban countryside, and not to one

12

of those abominable and abhorrent deserts of
paved streets laid out at right angles, and all
supplied with sewers and electric light wires
and water-mains before the first lonely house
escapes from the house-pattern books to tempt
the city dweller out to that dreary, soulless
waste which has all the modern improvements
and not one tree. I take it, I say, that you
are going to no such cheap back-extension of
a great city, but that you are really going
among the trees and the water-courses, sever-
ing all ties with the town, save the railway's
glittering lines of steel—or, since I have
thought of it, I might as well say the railway
ties.

If that is what your intent is, and you carry
it out firmly, you are going to a life which you
can never like, but which you may learn to
love.

How should it be possible that you should
enjoy taking up a new life, with new surroundings, new anxieties, new responsibilities, new
duties, new diversions, new social connections
—new conditions of every kind—after living
half a lifetime in New York ? It is true that,

being a born New Yorker, you know very
little indeed of the great city you live in. You
know the narrow path you tread, coming and
going, from your house to your office, and
from your office to your house. It follows, as
closely as it may, the line of Broadway and
Fifth Avenue. The elevated railroads bound
it downtown; and uptown fashion has drawn a
line a few hundred yards on either side, which
you have only to cross, to east or to west, to
find a strange exposition of nearsightedness
come upon your friends. Here and there you
do, perhaps, know some little by-path that
leads to a club or a restaurant, or to a place of
amusement. After a number of books have
been written at you, you have ventured timo-
rously and feebly into such unknown lands as
Greenwich Village; or that poor, shabby,
elbowing stretch of territory that used to be
interesting, in a simple way, when it was
called the French Quarter. It is now supposed to be the Bohemian Quarter, and rising
young artists invite parties of society-ladies to
go down to its table d'hôte restaurants, and see
the desperate young men of the bachelor-apart-

ments smoke cigarettes and drink California
claret without a sign of trepidation.

As I say, that is pretty near all you know
of the great, marvellous, multitudinous town

you live in—a city full of strange people, of
strange occupations, of strange habits of life,
of strange contrasts of wealth and poverty; of a
new life of an indescribable crudity, and of an

old life that breeds to-day the very atmosphere of the historic past. Your feet have never strayed in the side paths where you might have learned something of the infinite and curious strangeness of this strange city.

But, after all, this is neither here nor there. You have accustomed yourself to the narrow dorsal strip that is all New York to you. Therein are contained the means of meeting your every need, and of gratifying your every taste. There are your shops, your clubs, your libraries, your schools, your theatres, your art-galleries, and the houses of all your friends, except a few who have ventured a block or so outside of that magic line that I spoke of a little while ago. And now you are not only going to cross that line yourself, but to pass the fatal river beyond it, to burn your boats behind you, and to settle in the very wilderness. And you ask me if you will like it!

No, Modestus, you will not. You have made up your mind, of course, to the tedium of the two railway journeys every weekday, and when you have made friends with your fellow-commuters, you will get to like it, for

your morning trip in will take the place with
you of your present afternoon call at your
club.   And you are pretty sure to enjoy the
novelty of the first few months.   You have
moved out in the spring, and, dulled as your
perceptions are by years of city life, you cannot fail to be astonished and thrilled, and perhaps a little bit awed, at the wonder of that
green awakening.   And when you see how the
first faint, seemingly half-doubtful promise of
perfect growth is fulfilled by the procession of
the months, you yourself will be moved with
the desire to work this miracle, and to make
plants and flowers grow at your own will.   You
will begin to talk of what you are going to do
next year—for you have taken a three years'
lease, I trust—if only as an evidence of good
faith.   You will lay out a tract for your flower
garden and your vegetable garden, and you
will borrow your neighbor's seed-catalogue,
and you will plan out such a garden as never
blossomed since Eden.

And in your leisure days, of course, you *will*
enjoy it more or less.   You will sit on your
broad veranda in the pleasant mornings and

listen to the wind softly brushing the tree-tops
to and fro, and look at the blue sky through
the leaf-framed spaces in the cool, green
canopy above you; and as you remember the

cruel, hot, lifeless days of summer in your
town house, when you dragged through the
weeks of work that separated you from the
wife and children at the sea-side or in the
mountains—then, Modestus, you must look
upon what is before you, and say: it is good.

It is true that you can't get quite used to the sensation of wearing your tennis flannels at your own domestic breakfast table, and you cannot help feeling as if somebody had stolen your clothes, and you were going around in your pajamas. But presently your friend—for of course you have followed the trail of a friend, in choosing your new abode—your friend drops in clad likewise, and you take the children and start off for a stroll. As the pajama-feeling wears off, you become quite enthusiastic. You tell your friend that this is the life that you always wanted to lead; that a man doesn't really live in the city, but only exists; that it is a luxury to breathe such air, and enjoy the peaceful calm and perfect silence. Away inside of you something says that this is humbug, for, the fact is, the perfect silence strikes you as somewhat lonesome, and it even scares you a little. Then your children keep running up to you with strange plants and flowers, and asking you what they are; and you find it trying on the nerves to keep up the pretence of parental omniscience, and yet avoid the too-ready corrections of your friend.

" Johnny-jumper!" he says, scornfully, when you have hazarded a guess out of your

meagre botanical vo- cabulary: " Why, man, that's no Johnny-jumper, that's a wild geranium." Then he addresses himself to the other inquiring youngster: "No, my boy, that's not a chestnut; that's an acorn. You won't get chestnuts till the fall, and then you'll get them off the chestnut trees. That's an oak."

And so the walk is not altogether pleasant for you, and you find it safest to confine your remarks on country life to generalizations concerning the air and the silence.

No, Modestus, do not think for a moment that I am making game of you. Your friend would be no more at home at the uptown end of your little New York path than you are here in his little town; and he does not look on your ignorance of nature as sternly as you would look upon his unfamiliarity with your familiar landmarks. For his knowledge has grown upon him so naturally and unconsciously, that he hardly esteems it of any value.

But you can have no idea of the tragicocomical disadvantage at which you will find yourself placed during your first year in the country—that is, the suburban country. You know, of course, when you move into a new neighborhood in the city you must expect to find the local butcher and baker and candle-stick-maker ready to fall upon you, and to tear the very raiment from your back, until they are assured that you are a solvent permanency —and you have learned how to meet and repel their attacks. When you find that the same thing is done in the country, only in a differ-ent way, which you don't in the least under-stand, you will begin to experience a certain feeling of discouragement. Then, the humor-ous papers have taught you to look upon the Suburban Furnace as part of the machinery or property of a merry jest; and you will be shocked to discover that to the new-comer it is a stern and cold reality. I use the latter adjective deliberately and advisedly. There will surely come an awful night when you will get home from New York with Mrs. Modestus in the midnight train, too tired for anything but a drowsy chat by the lingering embers of the library fire over the festivities of the evening. You will open your broad hospitable door, and enter an abode of chill and darkness.

Your long-slumbering household has let fires
and lights go out; the thermometer in the
children's room stands at forty-five degrees,
and there is nothing for you to do but to
descend to the cellar, arrayed in your wedding
garments, and try your unskilful best to coax
into feeble circulation a small, faintly throb-
bing heart of fire that yet glows far down in
the fire-pot's darksome internals.   Then, when
you have done what you can at the unwonted
and unwelcome task, you will see, by the feeble
candle-light, that your black dress-coat is gray
with fine cinder dust, and that your hands are
red and raw from the handling of heavy imple-
ments of toil.   And then you will think of city
home-comings after the theatre or the ball; of
the quiet half-hour in front of the dying can-
nel; of the short cigar and the little nightcap,
and of the gentle passage bedward, so easy in
that warm and slumberous atmosphere that
you hardly know how you have passed from
weariness to peaceful dreams.   And there will
come to your spirit a sudden passion of humili-
ation and revolt that will make you say to
yourself: This is the end!

But you know perfectly well that it is *not* the end, however ardently you may wish that it was. There still remain two years of your un-subletable lease; and you set yourself, courageously and firmly, to serving out the rest of your time. You resolve, as a good prisoner, to make the best of it. You set to work to apply a l i t t l e plain common - sense to the problem of the furnace— and find it not so difficult of partial solution after all. You face your other l o c a l troubles with a determi- nation to mini- mize them at least. You re- solve to check your too open expressions of dissatisfaction with the life you are leading. You hardly

know why you do this, but you have, half-unconsciously, read a gentle hint in the faces of your neighbors; and as you see those kindly faces gathering oftener and oftener about your fire as the winter nights go on, it may, perhaps, dawn upon your mind that the existence you were so quick to condemn has grown dear to some of them.

But, whether you know it or not, that second year in the suburban house is a crisis and turning-point in your life, for it will make of you either a city man or a suburban, and it will surely save you from being, for all the rest of your days, that hideous betwixt-and-between thing, that uncanny creation of modern days of rapid transit, who fluctuates helplessly between one town and another; between town and city, and between town and city again, seeking an impossible and unattainable perfection, and scattering remonstrant servant-maids and disputed bills for repairs along his cheerless track.

You have learned that the miseries of country life are not dealt out to you individually, but that they belong to the life, just as the

troubles you fled from belong to the life of a
great city. Of course, the realization of this
fact only serves to make you see that you erred
in making so radical a change in the current of
your life. You perceive only the more clearly
that as soon as your appointed time is up, you
must reëstablish yourself in urban conditions.
There is no question about it; whatever its
merits may be—and you are willing to concede
that they are many—it is obvious that country life does not suit you, or that you do not
suit country life, one or the other. And yet—
somehow incomprehensibly—the understanding that you have only shifted the burden you
bore among your old neighbors has put a
strangely new face on things, and has made
you so readily tolerant that you are really a
little surprised at yourself.

The winter goes by; the ever welcome glory
of the spring comes back, and with it comes
the natural human longing to make a garden,
which is really, although we treat it lightly, a
sort of humble first-cousin to the love of children. In your own breast you repress this
weakness. Why taste of a pleasure which in

another short year you mean to put permanently out of your reach? But there is no

resisting the entreaties of your children, nor your wife's ready interest in their schemes, and you send for Pat Brannigan, and order a garden made. Of course, it is only for the children, but it is strange how readily a desire to please the little ones spreads into a broader benevolence. When you look over your wife's list of plants and seeds, you are surprised to find how many of them are perennials. "They will please the next tenants here," says your wife; "think how nice it would have been for us to find some flowers all already for us, when we came here!" This may possibly lead you to reflecting that there might have been something, after all, in your original idea of suppressing the gardening instinct.

But there, after a while, is the garden—for these stories of suburban gardens where nothing grows, are all nonsense. True, the clematis and the moonflower obstinately refuse to clothe your cot with beauty; the tigridia bulbs rot in the ground, and your beautiful collection of irises produces a pitiful pennyworth of bloom to an intolerable quantity of leaves. But the petunias and the sweet-williams, and the balsams, and all the other ill-bred and obtrusive flowers leap promptly into life and vigor, and fight each other for the ownership of the beds. And the ever-faithful and friendly nasturtium comes early and stays late, and the limp morning-glory may always be counted upon to slouch familiarly over everything in sight, window-blinds preferred. But, bless you dear urban soul, what do *you* know about the relative values of flowers ? When Mrs. Overtheway brings your wife a bunch of her superbest gladioli, you complacently return the compliment with a half-bushel of magenta petunias, and you wonder that she does not show more enthusiasm over the gift.

In fact, during the course of the summer you have grown so friendly with your garden that, as you wander about its tangled paths in the late fall days, you cannot help feeling a twinge of yearning pain that makes you tremble to think what weakness you might have been guilty of had you not already burned your bridges behind you, and told the house agent that nothing would induce you to renew the lease next spring. You remember how fully and carefully you explained to him your position in the matter. With a glow of modest pride you recall the fact that you stated

your case to him so convincingly, that he had
to agree with you that a city life was the only
life you and your family could possibly lead.
He understood fully how much you liked the
place and the people, and how, if this were
only so, and that were only the other way, you
would certainly stay. And you feel if the
house agent agrees with you against his own
interest, you must be right in your decision.
Ah, dear Modestus! You know little enough
about flowers; but oh, how little, little, little
you know about suburban house agents!

Let us pass lightly over the third winter.
It is a period of hesitation, perplexity, expectancy, and general awkwardness. You are, and
you are not. You belong nowhere, and to no
one. You have renounced your new allegi-
ance, and you really do not know when, how,
or at what point you are going to take up the
old one again. And, in point of fact, you
do not regard this particular prospect with
feelings of complete satisfaction. You remember, with a troubled conscience, the long list
of social connections which you have found it
too troublesome to keep up at long range. I

say you, for I am quite sure that Mrs. Modestus will certify me that it was You and not
She, who first declared that it was practically
impossible to keep on going to the Smith's
dinners or the Brown's receptions. You don't
know this, my dear Modestus, but I assure
you that you may take it for granted. You
remember also that your return must carry
with it the suggestion of the ignominy of
defeat, and you know exactly the tone of
kindly contemptuous, mildly assumed superiority with which your friends will welcome you
back. And the approaching severance of your
newer ties troubles your mind in another way.
Your new friends do not try to dissuade you
from going (they are too wise in a suburban
way for that), but they say, and show in a
hundred ways, that they are sorry to think of
losing you. And this forbearance, so different from what you have to expect at the other
end of your moving, reproaches and pains
while it touches your heart. These people
were all strangers to you two years and a half
ago; they are chance rather than chosen companions. And yet, in this brief space of time

—filled with little neighborly offices, with faithful services and tender sympathies in hours of sickness, and perhaps of death, with simple, informal companionship—you have grown into a closer and heartier friendship with them than you have ever known before, save with the one or two old comrades with whose love your life is bound up. When you learned to leave your broad house-door open to the summer airs, you opened, unconsciously, another door; and these friends have entered in.

.   .   .   .   .   .

It is a sunny Saturday afternoon in early April, but not exactly an April afternoon, rather one of those precocious days of delicious warmth and full, summer-like sunshine, that come to remind us that May and June are close behind the spring showers. You and Mrs. Modestus sit on the top step of your front veranda, just as you sat there on such a day, nearly three years ago. As on that day, you are talking of the future; but you are in a very different frame of mind to-day. In a few short weeks you will be adrift upon a sea of domestic uncertainty. For weeks you have visited the noisy city, hunting the proud and lofty mansion and the tortuous and humiliating flat, and it has all come to this—a steam-heated "family-hotel," until such time when you can find summer quarters; and then, with the fall, a new beginning of the weary search. And then—and then——

Coming and going along the street, your friends and neighbors give you cheery greeting, to which you respond somewhat absent-mindedly. You can hear the voices of your children and their little neighbor-friends playing in the empty garden plot. Your talk flags. You do not know just what you are thinking about; still less do you know what your wife is thinking about—but you know that you wish the children would stop laughing, and that the people would stop going by and nodding pleasantly.

And now comes one who does not go by. He turns in at the gate and walks up the gravel path. He smiles and bows at you as if the whole world were sunshine—a trim little figure, dressed with such artistic care that there is cheerfulness in the crease of his trousers and suavity in his very shirt-front. He greets Mrs. Modestus with a world of courtesy, and then he sits confidentially down by your side and says: " My dear sir, I am come to talk a little business with you."

No, you will not talk business. Your mind is firmly made up. Nothing will induce you to renew the lease.

" But, my dear sir," he says, with an enthusiasm that would be as boisterous as an ocean wave, if it had not so much oil on its surface: " I don't want you to renew the lease. I have a much better plan than that! I want you to *buy the house !* "

And then he goes on to tell you all about it; how the estate must be closed up; how the house may be had for a song; and he names a figure so small that it gives you two separate mental shocks; first, to realize that it is within your means; second, to find that he is telling the truth.

He goes on talking softly, suggestively, telling you what a bargain it is, telling you all the things you have put out of your mind for many months; telling you—telling you nothing, and well he knows it. Three years of life under that roof have done his pleading for him.

Then your wife suddenly reaches out her hand and touches you furtively.

" Oh, buy it," she whispers, huskily, " if you can." And then she gathers up her skirts and hurries into the house.

Then a little later you are all in the library, and you have signed a little plain strip of paper, headed " Memorandum of Sale." And then you and the agent have drunk a glass of wine to bind the bargain, and then the agent is gone, and you and your wife are left standing there, looking at each other with misty eyes and questioning smiles, happy and yet doubtful if you have done right or wrong.

But what does it matter, my dear Modestus ? For you could not help yourselves.

BOOKS BY H. C. BUNNER

"It is Mr. Bunner's delicacy of touch and appreciation of what is literary art that give his writings distinctive quality. Everything Mr. Bunner paints shows the happy appreciation of an author who has not alone mental discernment, but the artistic appreciation."—NEW YORK TIMES.

NOVELS AND SHORT STORIES

Jersey Street and Jersey Lane. ❧ ❧ ❧

Urban and Suburban Sketches. Illustrated by A. B. Frost, I. R. Wiles, and others. 12mo, $1.25.

Attractive and sympathetic sketches, alternating in scene between New York and the country. The little study of the East side, "Jersey and Mulberry," is as perfect as the purely pastoral "Story of a Path," and the humor of "A Letter to Town," and some of the other sketches, is as fine as the serious note of "The Lost Child," which contains some of Mr. Bunner's best work. The illustrations are numerous and exquisitely sympathetic.

The Story of a New York House. ❧ ❧ ❧

Illustrated by A. B. Frost. 12mo, $1.25.

"It is a great pleasure to come upon a piece of fine, conscientious work like this little story of Mr. Bunner's, which shows in every page a true artistic feeling. We value it not only for the neatness and grace of the style, but for the symmetry of the construction, just balance of sentiment, and an indefinable beauty of tone which is perfectly sustained from the first page to the last."—New York *Tribune*.

BOOKS BY H. C. BUNNER

Zadoc Pine. ❧ ❧

And Other Stories. 12mo, paper, 50 cents ; cloth, $1.00.

" They have all the best of his bright and attractive genius."—Chicago *Herald*.

The Midge. ❧ ❧

12mo, paper, 50 cents ; cloth, $1.00.

" The Midge is indeed a delightful creation, a dainty, fascinating, and original little story."—*The Critic*.

TWO VOLUMES OF VERSE

" *His verse pleased both the critical and the uncritical. It has the form, the finish, the flavor of scholarship that the cultivated recognize and relish ; and it has also the freshness, the spontaneity, the heartiness, and the human sympathy without which no poetry has ever been welcome outside the narrow circle of the dilettanti.*—MR. BRANDER MATTHEWS.

Airs from Arcady ❧ ❧ ❧

And Elsewhere. 12mo, $1.25.

" This is one of the cleverest and happiest volumes of verse that America has sent us for many years. In its brightness, its humor, its pathos, and its general hold of reality, it is often truly delightful. There is not a poem in the collection that has not its own peculiar merit."

—London *Academy*.

Rowen ❧ ❧ ❧

Second Crop Songs. 12mo, $1.25.

" Mr. Bunner sustains well his reputation as a poet who can turn from one meter to another and quite different one, and from one theme to another of a very dissimilar character, and show an equal mastery of each."

—*The Congregationalist*.

CHARLES SCRIBNER'S SONS, - NEW YORK